KEITH: FIREBRAND COWBOYS

BARB HAN

TORJAKE PUBLISHING

Copyright © 2023 by Barb Han

All rights reserved.

No part of this book may be reproduced in any form or by any electronic or mechanical means, including information storage and retrieval systems, without written permission from the author, except for the use of brief quotations in a book review.

Editing: Ali Williams

Cover Design: Jacob's Cover Designs

Proofreading: Judicious Revisions

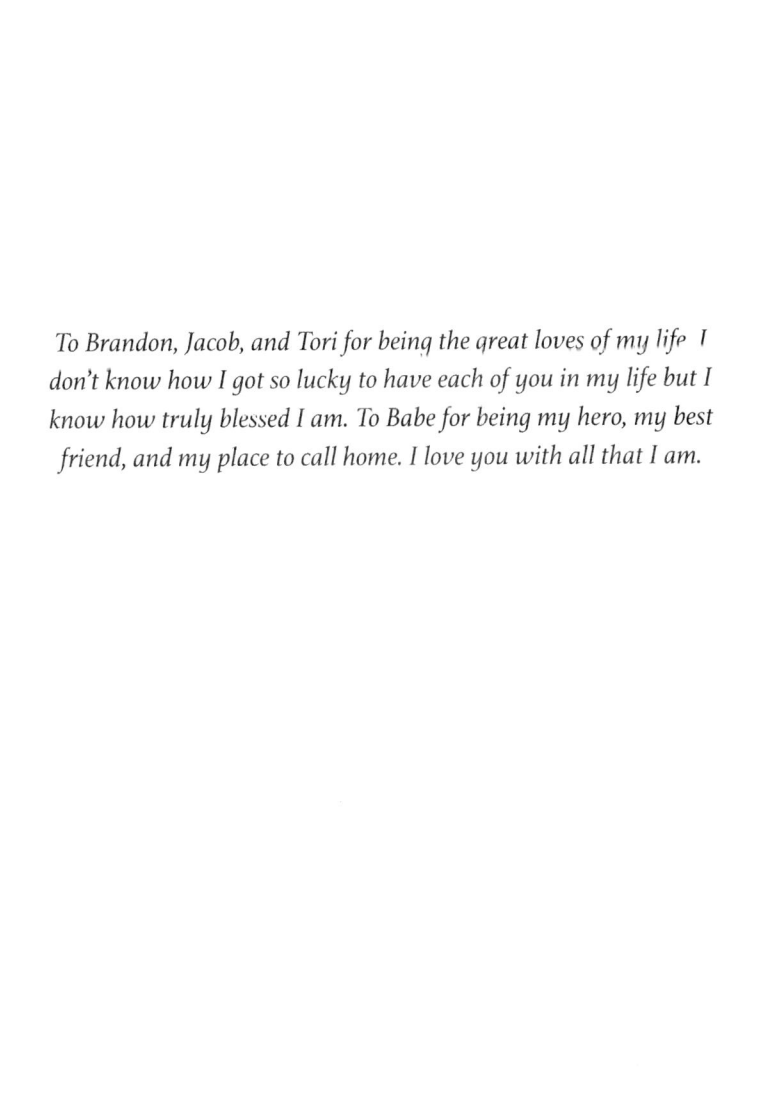

To Brandon, Jacob, and Tori for being the great loves of my life. I don't know how I got so lucky to have each of you in my life but I know how truly blessed I am. To Babe for being my hero, my best friend, and my place to call home. I love you with all that I am.

1

Amaya Katz blinked twice at the handsome young —emphasis on the word *young*—cowboy standing at the doorway, shaking his head. She immediately shifted her gaze to her brother, who stood next to said cowboy, before picking up her overnight bag. "Absolutely not."

Killian folded his arms over his chest, unfazed by her distress. He waved a hand in the air. "I realize these...*conditions*...aren't exactly what you're used to from your downtown Dallas apartment, however—"

"I don't mind sleeping in a barn," Amaya retorted before motioning toward the cowboy. She'd slept in far worse conditions. In fact, for most of her life she slept on a lumpy mattress on the floor close enough to a wall she could hear mice scurrying around in the evenings. Those conditions were luxury compared to the months she had little more than a thin blanket between her and a dirty carpet after coming home to find a deadbolt and eviction notice on the door. "But I do take issue with someone barely out of high school being my bodyguard."

"First off, my name is Keith Firebrand," the guy said, twisting his face up like he'd just sucked on a whole pack of Sour Patch candy. The disdain that followed aged his baby face up a few years. He had a young River Phoenix look about him. This cowboy was a taller, more muscled version of the late actor. "And secondly, I'm more than capable of offering the protection you need."

"What do you know about my situation?" Amaya asked, undeterred. Her brother Killian was trying to help, but this couldn't possibly be the answer. If her childhood had been awful, Killian's had been even worse. He's suffered the same sleeping conditions before his stint in jail, where he'd joked the mattress was off the floor at least. Other than saying that, he didn't open up about his time in lockup but it changed him.

"Look, ma'am. I'll be real honest with you," Keith started. "I don't know much about your current predicament. But that doesn't mean I—"

"He's more than up for the job," Killian interrupted. Her brother had good intentions but this was her life they were talking about. Someone tried to drug her in order to kidnap her to do God knew what. This was not a drill.

"You know what happened to me," she said to her brother. "And how much worse it could have been."

"I'm only sorry I wasn't there to stop it," Killian said with a frown and a headshake. Her older brother always took responsibility for everything that happened in life. Even at nineteen years old when him and three friends decided to pull something stupid for quick money by robbing a small convenience store on the outskirts of Fort Worth, he'd been the one caught while helping a buddy over the fence. He refused to give up the names of his friends. The judge had seen the move as an act of rebellion and gave Killian a harsher sentence. Five years behind bars for trying to steal four hundred and eighty-eight dollars. The incident had been classified as aggravated robbery because one of Killian's friends had pulled out a paintball gun and threatened the young guy behind the counter with it. The store worker couldn't tell the difference because, admittedly, those guns looked like the real thing. Thus, the officer on the scene reported the incident as an aggravated robbery. Since it was Killian's first offense, his sentencing was considered lenient. Five years of his life gone. That didn't sound lenient to Amaya.

"Not your fault," she pointed out to her brother, wishing he didn't hold the world on his shoulders. Five years in jail had changed him. In the years since, he'd bounced around trying to find work. Since convicted felons weren't exactly in high demand in the regular job market, he'd looked for alternative ways to make an honest living.

"None of this would have happened if I hadn't shown you the ropes," Killian countered. "I literally walked you right into this...mess. And I'd never be able to forgive myself if anything happened to my baby sister." He threw his hands up in the air and paced in the small space. One thing was certain, she wouldn't get lost going to the bathroom. It was literally attached to the eight-by-eight room where they stood. The space didn't bother her. The sawdust on the floor wasn't an issue. The cowboy, however, couldn't possibly get the job done.

"You're only four years older than me, Killian."

"Age doesn't matter," Killian defended. She looked over at Babyface and made a harrumph noise while tapping the toe of her high heel boots. "You know what I mean."

Amaya had no plans to relent. In fact, she intended to climb back into her Range Rover with the tinted windows and drive as far away from Firebrand Cattle Ranch as possible. With money drying up from her biggest sponsor, it was only a matter of time before the repo man would be paying a visit to take away her baby; the car she'd nicknamed Black Beauty after her favorite movie, shortened to Beauty. "Tell me why we're here at this ranch and why you think it's a good idea for this calf roper to be my entire security team." She glanced over at Keith, who had a bemused look on his face. "No offense."

"None taken," Keith quipped. Hands over his head, he gripped the doorjamb in a show of muscle.

The urge to wipe the shit-eating grin off his face struck like a fastball out of nowhere on a sunny day.

"This man happens to be one of the best at tracking poachers and—"

"Last time I checked, I wasn't trying to steal anyone's cows," she interrupted. Admittedly, it wasn't exactly a fair response, but her life had been threatened and she knew better than to brush it off or take it lightly.

Keith chuckled a low rumble underneath his breath that sent goosebumps up her arms. His presence had an unsettling effect and she didn't have time or energy to fight it.

Amaya shot him a warning look. "I'm not sure what about this situation amuses you but that's just one more reason for me to hop into Beauty and get the hell out of here."

"Don't make a rash decision, Amaya," Killian warned. "At least hear what I have to say first."

She paused, glaring at Babyface, and then nodded for her brother to go ahead.

"Poachers are some of the most slippery and dangerous criminals in Texas," Killian started. "Keith is one of the best trackers. Some say he knows how poachers think and that's the reason. This man is a legend in these parts."

Amaya opened her mouth but her brother put a hand up to stop her from speaking.

"I heard what you said about that not making him qualified to protect you as a security guard, but I think you're wrong about that," Killian argued.

"Are you willing to bet my life on your hunch?"

Killian stood there for a long moment, looking like he was carefully choosing his next words. "No one is going to look for you here, Amaya."

She couldn't argue his point there. The person who'd tried to drug her latte at a party that was supposed to seal the deal with a big sponsor wouldn't think to drive out in the middle of Cow Town Nowhere, USA, to find her. "Do you even get cell coverage out here?"

"Does it matter?" Keith asked, grin securely in place. She'd never been so attracted to someone she equally wanted to scream at before. This was new. She didn't like the conflicting feelings battling it out for control inside her. She didn't have time for the distraction.

She balled a fist and placed it on her hip. Keith's gaze followed, lingering on her curves, causing a trill of awareness to shoot through her. "How will I know when it's safe to come out of hiding if I can't reach my brother?"

"I'll be in contact with Killian."

The thought of being totally cut off from the world caused her chest muscles to constrict. Breathing hurt.

"That's not going to work for me," she said, shaking her head.

"There's a witch hunt going on out there for you, Amaya," Killian interjected. "Staying on the downlow is the only way to ensure your safety, sis. Having and using a cell phone or computer opens a door for a savvy hacker to find you. Is that what you seriously want?" More of that guilt crossed Killian's features. "Because it scares the hell out of me." He took a step toward her and reached for her hand. "Please, sis. Consider sticking around. For my sake."

Amaya wasn't trying to give her brother a hard time or stress him out. But there had to be a better way. Staying around here without any way to reach the outside world could make her a sitting duck. Besides, her skyrocketing internet success was falling almost as quickly as she'd risen. Without a way to stay connected to her followers, she had no way to repair her damaged image, regroup, and recoup her losses.

After someone posted a video of her half-dressed, makeup smudged holding onto an empty champagne bottle with the caption: *Sleeping her way up the ladder instead of working for it? Not cool!*

The internet went after her like a pack of angry dogs following the smell of fear.

"Hey, Princess," Keith said, stirring up a hornet's nest inside her with his tone and word choice. "Let me break it down for you."

Words tripped on her angry tongue or she would tell him what she really thought about being called a princess and how it felt to walk around in a fog half-dressed in downtown Dallas with no clear memory of what happened other than escaping and deathly afraid.

"You're broke," Keith pointed out without a hint of compassion. "I'm trying to start a side hustle. The way I see it. You need me more than I need you. But a high-profile case like yours is a good place for me to start."

White hot anger coursed through Amaya's veins. She

needed to grit her teeth and bear it. Keith was right. And she didn't have a better plan.

∼

KEITH WANTED to take this case about as much as he wanted to eat a bowl full of worms. Killian had mentioned his sister might not be—what had he said exactly?—*keen* on the idea of lying low at a cattle ranch. Despite being born and raised in Texas, she was as outdoorsy as a Pomeranian. Both would end up prey in a heartbeat.

Amaya turned to her brother, effectively placing her back to Keith. "Where are you going if I stay and how will I remain connected to the outside world?"

Keith had been blunt with his words, but Amaya needed to hear the truth. Killian had been upfront about her lack of ability to pay. Keith would be doing this work pro bono in order to build a reputation. Apparently, Amaya Katz was a big deal. Her star was on the rise in a field he admittedly knew nothing about…social media stars. "I'll take you to the main house once a day so you can check on anything urgent. I've got a guy who can scramble the cell towers so you won't be traced back here. But you have to use my equipment and give up your phone."

Other than a basic idea of how her business worked, he knew very little about her world. The internet was useful for keeping a website, ordering supplies, and logging the herd. Website updates and maintenance were out of his wheelhouse. He preferred to leave the computer work to someone who liked to sit at a desk. Keith loved open skies and being out on the land.

The feud his family had been involved in over the years had been between his older siblings and cousins. Being the youngest on his side of the family, he'd been able to stay out of it. Being on the land had been his safe haven from a spiteful grandfather and a father and uncle who'd spent their lives in petty competition with one another. The fallout was still being felt by Keith's generation. In fact, it had only heated up following his grandfather's recent death.

"This is the best place for you right now," Killian explained.

Keith's job was to protect Amaya but he also fully intended to launch his own investigation into who had targeted her, and why.

The tall, slender beauty with caramel-colored skin and golden-brown eyes looked every bit a celebrity. She had on a sparkly halter-type shirt in an emerald color, and slacks that flared. High heel boots weren't practical on the ranch. Those would have to go.

Amaya had an overnight bag. Did she have practical shoes inside? Jeans and a t-shirt? He doubted it. She was taller than his sisters-in-law or he'd borrow appropriate clothing on her behalf.

Long earrings could easily get hooked and tear a hold in her ear. She had no background working a ranch, but she could learn. He planned to put her to work and figure out a way to help her blend in.

Keith almost laughed out loud.

A statuesque beauty like her would most definitely not disappear into the woodwork. She was striking and elegant, not exactly words that paired well with ranching and cattle.

A hard day's work did the soul good. Keeping her busy would help take her mind off everything she'd been through and would help the time pass. Looking at her with her designer handbag hanging off her shoulder, he didn't know how many fences she'd be able to mend or posts she'd be able to help dig, but surely he could find something for her to do while she was at Firebrand.

There was a positive to this whole situation. She had no idea who he was or that his mother was presently in jail for attempted murder in a plot to get more of the inheritance. Amaya had never heard of the Firebrand name, despite the family's wealth and notoriety. She didn't look at him like he was the devil's spawn following his mother's arrest and admission of guilt.

So there was that.

Keith would put Amaya to work and investigate her case while she lived in the barn.

"I can't sleep here," she pleaded with her brother. "This place makes me itch. All this hay around. You know I'm allergic to animals."

"Afraid isn't the same thing as allergic, Amaya," Killian explained like he was talking to a four-year-old. The look he shot his sister said they'd slept in a whole lot worse and survived.

Her muscles stiffened. "Alright then. Go ahead and leave. I'll figure it out on my own. I don't need your help."

"You know that's what I'm trying to do, right?" Killian asked. On his left forearm was a prison-looking tattoo. Had he served time?

Keith had questions for Amaya as soon as her brother left the two of them alone. In fact, it was time to nudge her brother to make his exit. "I'll take good care of her."

Amaya wheeled around on him, defiance blazing in her eyes. He half expected her to poke a finger in his chest based on her expression. "I can take care of myself, thank you very much."

He took a step back and released the doorjamb, dropping his hands to his sides. "Never said you couldn't. But it never hurts to have someone else watching your back."

She opened her mouth to speak but then clamped it shut. Those honey-brown eyes narrowed as she studied him. The woman was beautiful. He had to give her that. Spoiled? Absolutely. But drop-dead gorgeous, even when she was madder than a wet hen.

Keith wasn't here to win a personality contest. He'd been hired to ensure her safety until the bastard who'd drugged her and ruined her reputation was found and safely locked behind bars. There'd been escalating threats sent to her PO Box set up for fan mail. Threats to expose her for what she truly was, whatever that meant. When she didn't cower, she'd been drugged. Since she'd been 'exposed' as a fraud online, accused of sleeping around to get what she wanted, the death threats had apparently been pouring in both online and in her fan box. One of her fervent followers, Loralee Bedder, was high on the suspect list. She'd volunteered to work for free as Amaya's assistant in order to help build Amaya's base. Just as they were in talks for Loralee to start taking a salary, Amaya's career blew up. Comments on her social media page turned ugly.

Loralee didn't take lightly to Amaya being called out as a fraud. She'd written a scathing text before blocking Amaya and anyone associated with her.

"It's getting late," Killian said. "I better get on the road so I can get back to Dallas before midnight."

"Where are you staying?" Amaya asked.

"I was thinking your apartment made the most sense," Killian said. His eye had been twitching for the past ten minutes. Nerves? Was he afraid of his sister in some way? She was a strong female but Keith's immediate impression of her was good. Did Killian cower to his sister? Was he afraid she would cut him off financially once she got back on her feet?

Keith had a lot to learn about Amaya. There was no time like the present no matter how much of a closed book she seemed to be.

"I'll check on you through Keith," her brother said as he turned toward the door.

"Fine," Amaya said under her breath, resigned.

Killian disappeared and Keith had questions.

2

Amaya took two steps toward the makeshift bed and then plopped down in defeat. "Is there a fresh blanket anywhere around here?" The current one smelled like horse. She guessed it was horse. People were surprised to learn she was born in Texas, considering she didn't know how to ride or shoot a gun.

In Dallas—she always had to explain—people ate more sushi than steak, and shopping was considered cardio. Her city wasn't a vacation destination, but the vibrant downtown Arts District was a trendy place to live. She'd grown up inside the loop, meaning Loop 12, where homes were smaller and pricier than ones in the suburbs. Which was also the reason for the roach-infested apartments they'd grown up in because a house was too expensive.

She and her brother Killian had essentially brought themselves up, since their father worked late into the night, or morning, depending on how she looked at it. The two of them had different mothers but the same father, who'd lost his shirt in the nightclub business years ago. But not before riding high and having two children with women who

KEITH: Firebrand Cowboys

worked in clubs on Northwest Highway, meaning adult entertainers. Amaya's mother took off after childbirth and left no trace. Apparently, she didn't want to risk being found by her daughter later in life. All Amaya knew about the woman was her stage name, Desiree. Real original, considering the word that came out after dropping the last e.

At seventeen, Amaya had moved in with a boyfriend to get away from her father's temper. He'd developed a drinking problem too, which only exacerbated his hothead.

"Tell me the basics about you," Keith said, interrupting her revelry.

"Why do you need to know any more than you already do?" Yes, she was being defensive, but she didn't see the point of playing the get-to-know-each-other game when she would be out of here in a matter of days. Or sooner. Hopefully, sooner.

Keith shot a look. "Because it's my job to keep you safe."

"We're on the same page there." She had no intention of sharing her life story, a story she didn't talk about with anyone. Her last couple of boyfriends had pointed out they knew the same about her at six months of dating, as at day two. That was their problem as far as she was concerned. When she pointed out the fact, they'd called her coldhearted. Amaya had let them walk out without an explanation as to why she might shut her emotions off to the world. She let them go without telling them how devastated she'd been when her father had gone on benders and left six-year-old her and her ten-year-old brother alone in a filthy apartment for days on end.

Knowing her background would only make them feel sorry for her. She needed pity like she needed someone to poke her eyes out. Pity didn't pay the bills or provide the financial security she desperately needed.

"Do you plan to talk?" an annoyed sounding Keith asked.

"You know everything you need to know about me," she quipped, sitting with her back straight. Amaya didn't like the idea of giving out personal information to a stranger. He might be tall and look stronger than an ox but he was no match for a bullet.

"Who is angry with you right now?" he pressed, unfazed by her protest.

"A long list of people," she said, figuring he would give up if he knew how many threats she'd received. "Dallas PD is looking into the attempt to drug me and sifting through the threats I've received by mail."

"Big city departments don't have a lot of resources to throw at finding a needle in a haystack," he reasoned.

"My brother argued the same thing," she admitted, keeping a physical distance from the far too good-looking for his own good cowboy.

"Did you shut down your blog, or social media app, or whatever the hell it is you run?"

"No," she stated. "I didn't. I'm on hiatus."

"Is it true you're broke?" This dude had a lot of personal questions—questions that struck a nerve.

How much could it hurt to tell him a little about what was going on? Besides, he made a good point about not being able to protect her if he couldn't identify the real threat. As long as they kept the conversation to business talk, she didn't see any harm in supplying information. "My biggest sponsor pulled the contract we were about to sign, saying they didn't do business with a fraud."

"Do you live paycheck to paycheck?" He cocked an eyebrow.

"My job doesn't really work like that," she said, turning

toward him ready to give him the five-cent update. "I was just breaking out. Part of the schtick is to look more successful than you are."

"Fake it 'til you make it?"

"Something like that," she agreed. "Being seen as successful brings in more followers, which in turn converts to cash from sponsors. My biggest was going to be Wholesome Cosmetics Company until all this happened."

"Spell the rest out for me," he said, leaning against the doorjamb. "What was their problem with you?"

"Sponsors get skittish easily nowadays," she explained. "And followers turn on influencers a little too quick now too. Reputation is everything. Mine has been stained by saying I slept around to get where I am today, and now I have no idea if I'll be able to recover. I'm in debt up to my eyeballs and can't make this kind of money cleaning office buildings, which, apparently, is the only other thing I'm qualified to do."

"Sounds like you need to find out who is behind this as much as I want to," Keith reasoned.

"I want my reputation back," she said without hesitation. "And I need my business back. The longer this thing runs, the more it blows up in my face."

"Then, I'll ask again," he continued without missing a beat. "Who is your biggest competitor?"

"Joelle Mercer," she offered. "We were up for the same contract."

"Did you sign?"

She shook her head. "But I was about to."

"How did you get loans for an expensive SUV and a home?"

"It's all smoke and mirrors," she said. "Beauty is on a lease program and I rent my apartment, so basically, I don't own anything. I made an arrangement with a staging company for the furniture. When I made the deal, I was going to promote them on my channel once I hit a certain number of subscribers. Companies send me clothes, shoes, and purses as a beauty influencer. Now, they want everything back. No one wants to be associated with me."

"Can your image be repaired?" Keith asked. Looking into his eyes there was a story behind those words.

"I hope so," she said on a gasp. "Why? What would a cowboy know about upholding a public image?"

Bemused, he clamped his mouth shut. After starting to speak a second time, he shook his head. "Wouldn't you like to know."

Now, she was interested in hearing what he had to say. Why was he being secretive about his life? What could he possibly have to hide? "What aren't you telling me?"

"Don't think I didn't notice how easily you turned the tables just then," he said. "That's an age-old trick and I'm not letting you get away with it."

"Okay, smart guy," she said, trying her best not to be affected by the twinkle in those cobalt-blue eyes of his. "What do you want to know about me?"

"Friends?"

"My best friend's name is Marcus but I call him Marky," she admitted. Giving him a little information about herself couldn't hurt.

"Where is he now?"

"Probably at his apartment or working his waitstaff job at Dakotas in downtown Dallas," she supplied.

"My kitchen," he said, translating the restaurant name from Spanish to English.

Did he expect a gold star? "That's correct."

"Enemies?"

"Who doesn't have a few of those?" she asked.

"How about a list of names?" he continued.

"There are a few influencers who believe there's only a finite amount of sponsors and have accused me of coming in late and infringing on their 'turf'." She made air quotes with her fingers when she spoke the last word out loud, rolling her eyes as she did so.

Some people were born jerks.

∽

Keith was finally getting somewhere, but they had to move. "Grab your overnight bag and let's go."

Big honey-brown eyes stared back at him. "Excuse me?"

So far, Amaya hadn't been cooperative or thrilled at being here in the barn. She'd experienced trauma. Someone had tried to take her life and was after her livelihood. He didn't intend on taking chances, not even with her family.

"How many folks know you're here?" he asked, tapping the toe of his boot with impatience.

"My brother," she said as one eyebrow arched.

"That's one too many."

"You don't trust Killian?" Her voice was filled with shock as she asked the question.

"When it comes to your safety, I don't trust anyone," he defended. As far as he was concerned, Killian was a risk. Amaya was coming across strong and together, basically overconfident. As far as he could tell so far, it was an act that would probably fool most folks. Keith grew up around eight siblings and nine cousins along with countless ranch hands over the years. He considered himself somewhat of an expert in reading body language.

Amaya was putting up a strong front. She was in defensive mode. Considering forty-eight hours ago she'd been on top of the world, she was doing better than most in keeping it together. He couldn't blame her for being distrustful.

"Where are we going?" she asked. No, demanded was probably a better word to describe her question. Was she used to being in charge? Calling the shots?

He pulled a silk pillowcase out of his back pocket. It had been cut down to cover a human head. Tossing it toward her, he asked, "Trust me?"

The square material hit her shoulder before dropping at her feet.

"I don't know you from Adam," she started, before putting a hand up like she was stopping herself and the world around her. When she turned her head toward him, their gazes met. Locked. The person who flinched or spoke first lost.

Keith wasn't sure how long the standoff lasted. Killian was right. It was getting late. Work started at the ranch early. Four o'clock in the morning would come fast, so he hoped they didn't end up standing there in the barn until it was time for the morning meeting.

On a sharp sigh, Amaya dropped down and then picked up the head covering. "Do you seriously need me to wear this thing?"

"Wouldn't have given it to you if I didn't."

"You threw it at me," she pointed out. "Why? Are you afraid I'll bite if you get too close to me? Am I a caged animal now?"

Keith played off her comments like they didn't sting. He should have walked to her and handed the modified pillowcase to her, rather than throw it. As much as he could have sympathy for her situation, she was as prickly as a rose's stem. Beautiful on the surface, but don't try touching the stem.

Besides, if he took a step toward her, she might get the wrong impression in the small space. Hemming her in might have the effect of a cornered animal. If he was going to get information out of her, he had to find a way to get her to trust him.

Throwing a pillowcase at her and asking her to place it over her head without offering an explanation was a great move, Firebrand.

As far as first meets went, they weren't off to a real good start.

"I apologize for not stepping into the room and handing you the head covering," he started, softening his tone as best as he could. "The space is small and I figured you wouldn't like me crowding you about as much as you'd like to use sandpaper instead of a washcloth in the shower." Giving himself the image of her naked in his bathroom wasn't the brightest idea, either.

Way to be 0 for 2, Firebrand.

Amaya gave a slight nod as she kept suspicious eyes on him. It was clear she didn't trust anyone. He'd seen the look before. It ran a lot deeper than what was currently happening to her.

Starting his own security business as a side hustle—to develop a way of being independent of Firebrand money in the event it all disappeared—wasn't going to be as easy as he'd hoped. The protection part wasn't the problem. He knew exactly where he wanted to take Amaya, and the best way to keep her out of the public eye. Dealing with someone who clearly didn't want to be here was the more difficult part of the business. He hadn't anticipated a scenario like this one. In his mind, his clients would all be willing participants who were eager to stay alive. They would cooperate because they trusted him, considering they'd hired him to do a job.

This?

Being with Amaya was the exact opposite of how he saw this gig going. Keith needed a minute to regroup. He was certain of one thing, though. They needed to stay on the move for the first twenty-four hours.

Keith fired off a text to his oldest brother, Kellan, to explain he'd be mending the east fencing over the next couple of days, and not to expect him at the morning meetings. There was a shed over that way that would keep them out of the elements. It wasn't much but they could make do. No one liked to check the east fencing because of the ravine and hills. Digging posts in the dry soil was damn near impossible.

East near the ravine was the best option, if he wanted to isolate them. She might push back on the lack of internet out there but he hoped to convince her to give it up for at least twenty-four hours while her world calmed down.

Looking up from his screen, he caught her studying him.

"I'm not sleeping in a tent if that's what you're thinking," Amaya said with the kind of finiteness that said arguing would be pointless.

"Then, what do you suggest?"

"A real bed," she said, tensing like she was preparing for backlash. "A hotel in your name."

He was interested in hearing her out. "Why would we do that?"

"I want to get to the bottom of whoever was behind drugging me more than you and my brother combined," she said plainly. "If you take me out..." She waved a wild hand. "There, wherever that is, how are we supposed to investigate? I'll be isolated from everything and everyone I know while being eaten alive by mosquitos and whatever other creepy crawlies are out there." She involuntarily shivered. "I don't do nature."

Listening to her, taking her seriously might help him gain some trust.

"Those are good points," he said. "But I'm curious to know why you thought I was going to take you out on the land."

She shot him a look. "Isn't that your plan?"

Keith chuckled. He couldn't help himself. "It was."

"Does that mean it isn't anymore?" she asked with the first real sound of hope in her voice that he might not screw up this job.

"Not now," he admitted. "So, what's our Plan B?"

Based on the spark in her eyes, he had a feeling she was about to lay it out for him.

3

The most expensive hotel in downtown Austin cost six hundred dollars a night on a weeknight in the off-season. Amaya had requested the best because no one would expect her or the cowboy Keith to stay here. It was the equivalent of hiding in plain sight. Amaya was a Dallas girl through and through. Despite Austin becoming less hippie and more hollow, she wouldn't be caught dead there.

Amaya involuntarily shivered at those last words—words that formed an echo inside her head. Someone out there actually wanted her dead. Dead or scared. Either way, the threat to her livelihood was real. She refused to go back to serving drinks in clubs, no matter how expensive the cover charge was or how much she made in tips. That money was chump change compared to what she was about to earn as a bonafide influencer, not to mention the growth potential. The cosmetic company was going to be just the beginning. The money she would have earned meant her first shot at real security, something she'd never known as a child. She craved the stability that would come with having

KEITH: Firebrand Cowboys 23

enough money in the bank to keep her from living on the streets. In her worst of times, she'd slept in the backseat of her dad's car. She'd gone to school smelling of body odor from lack of access to clean water for a shower and experienced the humiliation of being called down to the principal's office for it, not to mention the teasing.

Tears threatened at the memory, but Amaya sniffed them back and stuffed them down deep where they belonged.

The room in the most expensive hotel in downtown Austin was as plush and comfortable as she'd hoped it would be. A warm-toned chaise lounge was positioned in front of a window with a view of the capital building, a building that glowed at night and lit up the sky.

Since it looked comfortable and she wanted to look out the window, she took a seat there and unzipped, then kicked off her boots.

"How close are you and your brother?" Keith asked, taking the office chair on rollers at the nearby desk.

"We used to be tight," Amaya admitted, figuring Keith needed some background information in order to help her. "Thick as thieves as kids." She pinched the bridge of her nose as she focused on the dotting of stars. "But then it was just the two of us for a long time, so all we had was each other. And we got picked on a lot, so we had to team up."

Keith studied her but didn't give away his reaction. "Killian is the oldest, right?"

"By four years," she revealed. "But he matured a lot slower so it feels like I'm the oldest sometimes." Amaya sat up and planted her feet on the plush carpeting. "We have the same dad but different moms, which maybe you already know."

She risked a glance at Keith, who shook his head. Were

all families as messed up as hers? Because on the outside, everyone else seemed normal by comparison.

"Both of our moms are...were...possibly still are...strippers," she explained without making eye contact. There was no way she planned to look Keith in the eyes after the admission. It always went the same. Men were interested in her. They asked her out. They got her talking about her family. They learned her mother was an adult entertainer. The way they treated Amaya changed. Suddenly, she didn't need to go out to dinner. The men asked to come over for drinks instead. She knew a booty call when she was asked for one. And, no, she wasn't that kind of woman. For whatever reason, call it a curse, she needed to have a strong emotional bond before she went to bed with a man. So, at twenty-five years old, she could still count the number of men she'd slept with on two fingers.

The way her dates changed was gross and wholly unfair but, sadly, reality. It also taught her the power of perception as well as the damage it causes. To represent a cosmetics company with a brand image that was clean and wholesome meant she needed to look and act the part.

"I'm sorry," Keith said with a kindness and compassion like she'd never known. His words wound through her, wrapping around her broken heart like a warm blanket on a cold night. They held her shattered pieces together in a way that almost made her feel whole again. Almost. Because going full tilt wasn't an option.

"It happens, right," was all she managed to say. All she could say. There was something uniquely intimate about this moment of sharing.

"Believe me when I say how unfair it is that it happened to you."

Why did she find this stranger's words so comforting?

"I'm an adult now," she reminded both him and herself. The small child who'd missed out on a mother's touch was long gone. Amaya was tough and self-reliant. She didn't need or rely on anyone.

And now that her reputation was smeared, all anyone had to do was dig into her background for the 'like mother, like daughter' comparisons to shred what was left of her.

Keith didn't speak. He sat there in the chair without judgment, which was a foreign response. Did he have pain in his background? Could she afford to care?

"Anyway," she said, shaking off the overwhelming feeling of calm that surrounded her when she was alone in a room with Keith. It had unnerved her in the barn to the point she'd become prickly. He didn't deserve it. "We don't pick our families, right?"

"Truer words have never been spoken," he said with a heaviness to his voice that said there was a story behind the comment. She had every intention of asking about his family later. If there was a later.

"My brother was in jail," she said. "Did you know that?"

Again, Keith shook his head. "Normally, I would run a background check on a new client but your case came in fast and hot, and I've been up to my ears in family problems of my own.

"It happened a long time ago," she explained. "But I don't think he's ever fully recovered."

"Mind telling me the charges?"

"He and some friends robbed a convenience mart on the outskirts of town. He was nineteen at the time and the only one who got caught. He stopped to help one of his friends over a fence and ended up being the one who got busted."

"I'm guessing he refused to give up his buddies," Keith said.

"That's right." She barely recognized her brother by the time he was released. "Killian served five years, which basically stole his youth."

"What about the other guys?"

"None of them so much as visited him in jail," she said with more anger than she'd intended. It was true, though. Not one darkened the door of the jail. "He defends them to this day, saying they were too scared. They were afraid the law would put two-and-two together and bust them."

"It doesn't work like that," Keith pointed out.

"No. But they were basically kids themselves. Although, to be fair, they should have turned themselves in. Killian got extra time because he refused to give up his accomplices." She tapped a balled fist on her knee. "None of it was his idea but he took the fall. He had a code that said he wouldn't tell on the others, but one of his friends brought the paintball gun, not him. It increased the charges."

"What about having a lawyer?" Keith asked.

"Our dad didn't have money to defend his son when we barely kept food in our stomachs. Lawyers are for rich people." She bit her bottom lip to keep from saying anything else. "Suffice it to say my brother paid the price for making a foolish mistake at a young age. He shouldn't have been involved at all but he was and it changed his life forever."

"I'm sorry to hear it," Keith said with more of that sincerity that had her believing he actually cared. "Kids make mistakes."

"They have to pay the piper, though," she said. "I'm not saying my brother should have gotten away with it. The clerk believed the paint gun was real. He believed his life was about to end. That's not fair, either."

"No, it isn't."

KEITH COULDN'T AGREE MORE. And yet there had to be some room for mistakes as kids. Grown adults, on the other hand, should know better, even if they'd had rough childhoods. Take his mother, for instance; she had no right attempting murder, no matter how difficult her upbringing had been. Going down that road in his mind only led to heartache, so he stopped himself right there. Shaking his head, he refocused. "Tell me more about how Killian's life was impacted by the arrest and jail time."

"You must know how impossible it is to get a job with a felony conviction on someone's record," Amaya explained.

At the ranch, they took in folks who were committed to change, no matter their past. On occasion, a bad seed slipped through the cracks. Overall, though, they expected a hard day's work in exchange for a day's pay. As long as someone was committed to change, they were hirable. Did the philosophy backfire sometimes? Hell, yes. Would Keith or his family have it any other way? No. Because more lives and futures were saved than lost. Ranch work was physical, hard, and good for the soul as far as Keith was concerned.

"Like I said, Killian came out a different person," Amaya continued with a wistful look in those mesmerizing honey-browns. "He stopped laughing. You know?" She twisted her hands together and bit down on her bottom lip. "Like really laughing. And his eyes lost that spark they once had. They were dull. He put up a brave front, but I knew him and I could tell he was broken. Trying to hold it together. He was harder too. Like, things that used to bother him didn't even hit the radar anymore. It was weird when I first saw him again. I'm used to it now though."

"Are you two still close?"

"Not like we used to be," she said on a shrug. "Distant is probably a good word to describe our relationship now. It's a good word to describe my brother too. He stopped smiling for the longest time, and when he finally did again, it came across as forced. It didn't reach his eyes, if that makes sense."

"It does," Keith reassured.

Amaya tapped her heel on the carpet a few times. "He's been lost ever since. Except recently. Maybe in the last year and a half. He started to liven up again."

"What made the difference?"

"Time, for one," she supplied. "He realized there might be money to be made on the internet. Started off by streaming the games he was playing. He made a little money there and figured he could grow his business." She glanced behind her into the night sky. "It's how I came up with the idea to become an influencer. Watching him gave me the idea. I started gaining traction almost immediately."

Killian was protective of his younger sister, which made sense. "What will your brother do to get to the bottom of who is trying to kill you?"

"That part scares me the most," she admitted. "Before jail, my answer would have been different. I knew him. After? It's like a new person walked out of the prison yard and got into my car the day I picked him up."

"What about your father?" Keith asked. He knew full well how parents influenced their children and how intensely the older generation affected lives. Without going into detail, he had intimate knowledge of how messed up parents screwed up their offspring.

The torch was even worse when generations handed down the fiery stick. And almost unimaginable when said generation not only took the torch but ran with it. The flame ignited into a devastating forest fire.

"Once Killian was locked up, our dad wrote him off as bad news," Amaya said, with eyes that pierced right through him. In a rare moment of vulnerability, he saw the depth of the pain there too. "I moved in with a boyfriend at seventeen and haven't seen the old man since."

"But you kept in touch with your brother."

"I couldn't visit him in jail until I turned eighteen," she said. "Even then, I could only manage to go once a month, if that." She dropped her gaze to the carpet. "A few of the times I went there, his eyes would be puffy like he'd been crying. Other times, he had a black eye and cuts on his face. Once, he refused visitation."

"Did he ever say why?"

"Nope," she admitted. "My brother started playing his hand close to his chest. I never asked either. I knew deep down that he didn't want to talk about what happened. If I'm being really honest, I didn't want to know. It was bad enough seeing what he looked like sometimes. Hearing the words would have only made it worse for me. So, yeah, I was a chicken. I hid from the truth."

Keith had a hard time imagining Amaya would hide from anyone or anything, so the admission caught him off guard.

"What's that look?" she asked, studying him.

"I'm surprised," he said. "You're strong-willed, so it's hard for me to see you in another light."

She opened her mouth to speak but he silenced her with a look of apology.

"You were a kid," he said. "I get it. People grow up. They change."

"I hated the feeling of being out of control." She balled her fists and placed them on top of her thighs. Tension lines formed on her forehead and in the form of brackets around her mouth—a mouth he had no business focusing on. "At some point in all that mess, I made a promise to myself that I wasn't going down that road again. The pain made me who I am. It made me stronger in a lot of ways. Not that I would wish it on anyone else."

"Sometimes life hands good people a crap hand," he offered. "All we can do is play the cards best we can. Learn. Try not to make the same mistakes over and over again."

"That's the truth."

The moment happening between them needed to calm down. Because for a second there, he thought they were forming a bond. Which meant it was time to change the subject before he could go down that rabbit hole.

"What about your best friend? The waiter?"

Amaya cocked her head to one side, looking caught off guard at the pivot. "What about him?"

"How close are the two of you?" Keith had yet to ask about a boyfriend. Part of him, a part that needed to be kept in check, wanted to know for more reasons than this case.

"He's my best friend. Why?"

"Have the two of you been in any disagreements lately?" Keith asked. It wasn't likely but he needed to cover every possible angle in order to hone in on who he wanted to speak to one-on-one.

"No," she said defensively. A little too defensively?

Keith had more questions about the best friend, along with a twinge of jealousy he had no business feeling.

Why was Amaya defensive about her best friend?

4

"I'm not going to sit here and pretend I've never been in an argument with my best friend." Amaya sat up straight and then crossed her legs, daring him to doubt her.

Keith studied her with laser-like eyes—eyes that pierced through her. She'd already told him more than any other human being, including her best friend. Keith had her off balance. Or maybe it was the situation. Yeah, she reasoned it had to be the circumstances and not because she felt chemistry between her and the rancher, despite the fact that he would light a fire inside any female he met. There was probably a whole line of women waiting in the wings for a guy like Keith. Other than being drop-dead gorgeous with a body that wouldn't quit, he came across as genuine.

Dallas was a more cosmopolitan city with plenty of rich people. Surrounding the city was University Park, Highland Park, and several other neighborhoods where a starter home broke through the million-dollar mark. She could admit there was a certain fakeness that came with the territory. Just north of Dallas was the Botox capital of the US, surpassing Los Angeles.

There was a lot of opportunity too. Opportunity to make something of herself instead of living paycheck to paycheck, and sometimes not making it that far, like her father had the last time she'd seen him. Amaya had blocked him on her social media account and her cell, just in case he tried to get hold of her and cash in.

What could she say? The man was no good and would use any means necessary to finagle his way back into her life, especially once he found out she was doing well. *Had* been doing well, she corrected.

When she glanced up at Keith, he was staring at her.

"What?" she asked a little defensively.

"You didn't answer my question," he said, calm as he pleased.

"Oh," she said. To say she'd been feeling off would be the understatement of the century. Then again, this was the first time someone had tried to take her life, so she wasn't exactly experienced at being someone's target. She didn't know the protocol for how she was supposed to feel. "Remind me what the question was again."

Keith smiled and it warmed the entire room. "You're tired and I'm putting you through a round of fifty questions. How about trying to get some sleep instead?"

"I couldn't if I tried."

"I'm about to make a cup of coffee," he said. "Want one?"

She scratched the top of her head. "Yeah. Sure. Why not."

Keith got up and retrieved a bottle of water. He caught her attention and tossed it toward her, gently this time. "Take that down first while I figure out this piece of modern machinery." He made a helpless face.

Amaya bit back a laugh. Turned out Keith had a sense of humor. "Do you want me to get up and help? Because I will."

"No." He waved her off. "If I can't figure this out, then I can't call myself a true coffee drinker, now can I?"

"Agreed on that point," Amaya said enthusiastically enough to get a side glance from Keith and a crooked smile. The break in tension was a relief. So much so, that she wanted to change into something more comfortable.

The bathroom was off the bedroom of the suite. "Mind if I change?"

"Go right ahead," he said with a crick in his throat. That caused Amaya to smile but she quickly suppressed it. She didn't want to get too comfortable with Keith. Their business relationship would be short-lived, or so she hoped because that would mean her life would be back on track quickly. Building momentum was everything to an influencer. Losing it meant climbing the hill all over again, praying for a miracle that caused her popularity to catapult. She had some damage control to do to her reputation once the danger was behind her.

Grabbing her overnight bag and heading toward the bathroom, she was still trying to process everything that had happened. Thank the heavens for Killian's quick thinking. He'd shown up out of nowhere, which was the reason she was still alive.

The bedroom had a king-size bed. The room, similar in look and feel to the living area, had a surprisingly soft and comfortable feel. The master bath was large, elegant. She could get used to a place like this. The soaking tub called her name but she didn't have time for a warm bath no matter how amazing it sounded.

Amaya changed into the velvet tracksuit she'd tucked

into her bag, along with a pair of fuzzy socks. After being in high-heeled boots for the past fourteen hours straight, socks felt amazing. It was the little pleasures in life, she'd noticed, in times of crisis. Those little peeks of normalcy provided a surprising amount of comfort.

She sat on the edge of the tub for a few minutes, taking turns rubbing each foot until the circulation came back. She'd slipped off her boots when she first sat on the chaise lounge in the living room and had no regrets.

Her mind circled back to the questions Keith had asked. He didn't know her or her friends. Correction, friend. Singular. Marky was it. He was her best friend and her only friend all wrapped up into one. The last boyfriend she'd had was…

Hold on. Seriously?

It took Amaya a minute to pull up the name. Had it really been that long she couldn't remember off-hand?

Landon Sheppard. He'd managed the waitstaff where she worked. The two had started a work romance that had fizzled out almost as fast as the fuse had been lit. He'd called her cold-hearted when she wouldn't drop everything to bring him soup when he caught a cold. She'd called him a child who was incapable of taking care of himself.

Both had been right.

Getting close to someone scared the crap out of her. She'd believed she could handle a relationship if they took it slow. Landon had been a bull in a China shop when it came to dating. He was the charge ahead, consequences be damned type.

Within a few weeks of dating, he'd dropped the L word. She was still trying to figure out how he knew he loved her in a matter of weeks. Since she took those words seriously, she hadn't been able to say them back.

In fact, she was pretty sure her response had been, "Thank you."

Cold hearted?

Maybe.

Honest?

Absolutely.

Landon had been nice enough, and there'd been enough of an attraction to say yes to getting to know each other outside of work, but in Amaya's mind, that would take months if not years. She was more the proceed-with-caution type.

Was that cold-hearted? Or just practical? Was that being too protective of her heart? Or just making certain she meant those words before she said them. They rolled a little too easy off Landon's tongue.

When he'd confronted her about her response a couple of days later, or should she say a couple of days' worth of pouting later, she'd decided to break off the relationship. He wanted more than she did. All she'd been capable of was casual dating. Landon, on the other hand, had been ready to move in together and say *those* words every night before sleeping in the same bed.

Amaya involuntarily shivered. She wished she could shake off the memory of the hurt look on his face when she'd ended it. She hadn't wanted to cause him hurt, but it would have done him far more harm if she hadn't been honest about how she felt. He deserved to be with someone who loved him back the same way.

Right now, she wanted to erase the past and figure out who had it out for her. After freshening up, she rejoined Keith in the living area of the suite. He handed over a fresh cup of coffee.

"I wasn't sure how you took yours," he said with an apologetic look on his face.

Unlike Landon, Keith was someone she could see herself with for the long haul.

Amaya blinked a couple of times trying to erase the mental image of the two of them together as a family before taking the offering. The brief image both scared and excited her for reasons she didn't, no couldn't, examine. She cleared her throat. "I like mine black."

∽

AMAYA HAD the kind of deep, soulful eyes that were like magnets. They made him want to lean in closer. So, rather than let himself get caught up in the pull, he forced himself to take a couple of steps away from her to reclaim the desk chair he'd been sitting in before he started fiddling with the coffee machine. It had been easy to figure out, unlike the woman sitting across the room from him.

This lady had what he'd heard others refer to as an old soul. The same had been said of Keith. He wasn't entirely sure what it meant, except to say he was wise beyond his years. Tell that to his fifth grade English teacher and he was pretty sure the response would be a belly laugh. Mrs. Crabapple had returned one of his writing samples with a giggle and a comment that had convinced him that he would never be much more than a rancher. Not that ranchers weren't smart. She meant that he was too ignorant to do anything besides the family business where he could be carried.

Damn. Where did that come from? Keith hadn't thought about Crabapple in years. He'd tucked her memory away long ago despite letting her reaction to him sit in the back of his mind longer than he cared to admit.

"You were telling me about your friend," he said, refocusing after taking a sip of the fresh brew. It wasn't half bad for hotel coffee. Granted, he preferred the tin can over a campfire method but this did the trick.

Amaya shrugged. "There isn't much to tell. Marky and I met working as waitstaff. He moved on to working at Dakotas where he..." He must have shot her a look because she stopped midsentence. "Dakotas is one of those elite restaurants where rich people eat. It's downtown. You know the type. It's a place to be seen, if you know what I mean."

Keith understood the concept, despite having zero personal experience with caring about being seen in a trendy restaurant. He preferred his dinners cooked much in the same way as his coffee, over an open flame. Steaks on the grill along with corn on the cob and a potato was his favorite meal. Being a cattle rancher had its perks, since Firebrand produced the best steak in Texas, in his not-so-humble opinion. The ranch was the one thing his grandfather had gotten right.

For that, the family owed the man some respect. As far as the Marshall's personal life was concerned...there he'd earned zero respect from his offspring and their descendants.

Was Keith being too hard on the man who'd pitted his sons—Keith's father and uncle—against each other from birth? The Marshall might have had a complicated upbringing but then so did Keith and the others. They'd turned out to be good people despite the handicap of parents messed up beyond recognition.

Why were they able to overcome the past when others in the family weren't? What made them so different? Special?

"How close are the two of you?" he continued, forcing his thoughts back to the present.

"We fight all the time and then make up," she supplied with a Cheshire cat kind of grin. "It's our thing. You know?"

"Nope," he admitted. "I don't." The relationship sounded more like frenemies than true friends. But then Keith saw things as black or white. He didn't do gray areas.

"Come on," she said, drawing out the words. "Are you telling me that you never get in a fight with your bestie?"

Keith laughed. He couldn't help it.

"Did I make a joke? Because you need to clue me in on what's funny." Her face twisted in confused frustration.

"My job keeps me out on the land for days on end," he explained. "The only folks I see work at the ranch and I haven't been on a date in..." He decided not to fill her in on just how desperate his life sounded. There hadn't been anyone of the opposite sex in too long because, frankly, he'd been bored out of his mind on the last few dates he'd been on. As much as Keith appreciated a beautiful woman, he needed something more than a pretty face to hold his interest. There was only so long a person could sit across another person in a booth without interesting conversation. Besides, at some point, the shine would wear off looking at beauty on the outside. Being with someone who had a unique take on life, who could hold her own and make him laugh was the standard. He'd tried sex for sex's sake once. Learned he could never do that again.

"Suffice it to say Marky and I always end up friends again," Amaya interjected when he didn't finish his sentence.

"I'm putting him on the list of folks I'd like to talk to."

"*Okayyyyy*, but I think you're barking up the wrong tree," she said. The way she drew out words shouldn't be as sexy as it was. With eyes he could stare into for days, her quirks only enhanced her attractiveness.

"Fine," he said. "He's last on the list. Is that better?"

"I'd only talk to him for ideas about other people," she stated after a thoughtful pause. "Marky always has my back and he may have picked up on a vibe." She took a sip of coffee. "It might be good to move him up the list after all."

Keith shot her a look that said, 'I told you so'.

"Got it," she said with an adorable eye roll. "Mia culpa. You got there faster than I did, didn't you?"

This didn't seem like the time to rub her nose in the fact he'd been right, so he didn't. "Doesn't matter as long as we're on the same page." The urge to protect her and spare her feelings was something he hadn't experienced in a long time. Keith tried to chalk it up to being good at his new line of work even though it didn't ring true.

"Okay, so we talk to Marky," she said then slapped her thigh. "Killian took my phone away so no one could track me. I don't know anyone's phone numbers. Everyone is just a name in my contacts to me. How sad is that?"

"It's normal," he said on a chuckle, trying to lighten the mood. Getting Amaya to relax meant getting more information from her. *Another lie?*

Keith *wanted* to get to know Amaya better. And if that little voice in the back of his mind would shut the hell up, he could convince himself the reason was purely professional. "Tell me more about your rivals."

5

The influencer world was more cutthroat than Amaya had realized it would be. Not in the beginning when her name blended in with all the others; she'd essentially been background noise the first year to year and a half, before she started gaining followers. As soon as her star had started to rise, the haters appeared almost like out of a fog where she didn't see them coming until they were right on top of her. "We're all up for the same contracts. My biggest competition for the makeup contract was someone who goes by the handle Puddin' Pop."

Keith's face twisted in disgust.

"I know. I know." She stuck her palms up and shrugged. "Gimmicks work. They gain followers. Followers equals sponsors, which equals money in the bank. It's an influencers bread and butter."

"Is Amaya Katz your real name?" Keith asked.

"Amaya is my first name." She hadn't intended to reveal her last name. "Both Killian and I changed our last names after our father stole Killian's identity and opened up a bunch of credit cards; cards which were charged to the hilt while Killian was behind bars."

"Damn."

"Damn is right," she agreed. "You probably can't relate to having such a screwed-up family. My father sank to some serious lows."

"You'd be surprised," Keith said low and under his breath.

She doubted it. Nothing shocked her anymore. At twenty-five years old, she was already jaded. Very few people got past her carefully constructed walls—walls that had come up during her childhood. She had no intention of dropping them now. Especially not with a stranger. The only reason she was giving up details of her personal life now was because someone was trying to erase her from the earth.

Amaya shivered involuntarily at the thought. It really was a dog-eat-dog world out there. She'd learned the lesson early in life but hoped it wasn't true.

"What's your last name?" Keith asked, breaking into her revelry.

"Peterman was our last name." She emphasized the word *was* just in case Keith didn't get the memo.

"Why Katz?"

She did the shrug move again. "Why not? It's cool and, besides, who doesn't love cats?"

"People who are allergic to them," he stated.

"Okay, fine," she said. "I'll give you that one. But face it. They get away with anything and everything in their homes. Cats are slave to no one. Dogs, as sweet as they are, wait endlessly for their owners to come home and pet them or give them attention. Cats could care less. As long as they have food, water, and a place to do their business, they're all set. They don't crave your approval."

Keith's smile was more like a smirk before he took a sip of coffee. It was cold by now but that didn't seem to bother him at all. Throw a couple of ice cubes in the mug and call it a day. "Cats are good at keeping menaces out of the feed in the barn."

Amaya made a face. "Mice?"

"Yep," he confirmed. "And you're right about them being independent. Barn cats have little use for affection. Although, there is a little tabby that likes the occasional head scratch."

"Can you blame it?" she mused.

"Have you ever tried to figure out the real name behind Puddin' Pop?" he asked.

"Not really," she said. "I've never done a true investigation because I didn't care all that much and I never really saw her as a threat. She did seem to know about my deal before it was confirmed. I can count on one hand how many people knew about the collaboration with Wholesome.

"I'm guessing your brother was one of the folks in the know," Keith started. "And my money is on your best friend as the second."

"How do you know the number was two?" she asked, genuinely curious.

"Because those are the only two names you've brought up," he pointed out.

"I have a virtual assistant too, but I highly doubt she figured out what was going on," Amaya said.

"What's her name?"

"Loralee Bedder," Amaya supplied.

"Tell me everything you know about her," he requested.

"We've never met in person," she said. "All I know about

how she looks is from her profile pic." She reached for her handbag before stopping herself. "Right. I don't have a cell phone or a laptop. Hand me yours."

Keith retrieved his cell before handing it over. "Fair warning. I don't have any of that social media stuff on my phone."

He took a seat next to her on the chaise. He smelled like a mix of sandalwood and cedar with a citrus finish. There was something earthy and intoxicating about his unique scent. Amaya had to force herself to stay put while she breathed him in. Instinct had her wanting to find a quick getaway, except there was something different about Keith that planted her feet to the floor. A growing part of her wanted to lean into it, into him. The draw to this man was unlike anything she'd experienced before.

But then, she'd never been in this situation before. Being drugged and almost—what? Killed? Was that what the person had intended?—was affecting her mental state. Her reaction to Keith couldn't be more than that. It had to be some weird brain science like she was searching for proof of life or her biology was causing her to be overwhelmingly attracted to the first available man. To be fair, Keith was more than just the next best thing. Even from their short interactions, she could see he was honest and sincere. He was smart, a quality that trumped all others. The few times he'd broken the tension with a comment or a half-smile had been water to drought. Not to mention he had that whole tall, dark, and handsome thing going on in spades.

"You don't need social media to look someone up," Amaya said as she typed in her personal assistant's name. "See."

A picture of a woman in her late forties popped up.

"What's your business arrangement?" he asked as he

studied the screen, taking in the middle-aged woman's features.

"She approached me early on in my career, wanting to help get my brand off the ground," Amaya said. "I was already gaining some traction, and she'd been following me from almost day one."

"Interesting," he said, as casual as anyone pleased. Sitting next to her didn't seem to be having the same effect on him as it was on her. He came across as completely unfazed by their closeness; meanwhile, she flexed and released her fingers a few times on her free hand to stop from reaching for him.

"We worked out a deal that's not uncommon in the social media world," she continued. "Loralee worked for no pay in the early days, and then I started her on a small salary. She was working for other influencers at the time so these exchanges were how she brought new business on board. As soon as I could pay, we started with minimum wage and worked our way up from there. With this deal, she was about to be on a livable salary."

He nodded.

She realized Keith had taken the same type of arrangement in order to get his personal security business off the ground.

"In theory, this picture could come from any random place on the internet," he surmised after a thoughtful pause. He'd set his coffee cup down on the desk. Hers was already empty.

Amaya's stomach picked that moment to growl. She tried to cover with a cough. "That's true. I've never laid eyes on the woman, despite feeling very much like I know her."

"That's the trick of the internet, isn't it?" he asked but the question was rhetorical. "You hear about pedophiles grooming kids for months before making a move, convincing their targets they are the same age. They find ways to make them comfortable with similarities and such. Or so the news has said." He put a hand up before she could protest. "I'm not saying it's the case here but it's something to consider."

Loralee didn't show up until Amaya started having some success. That was true enough. Wouldn't Amaya have been savvy enough to ferret out a fake? Considering her upbringing, she'd had a lot of experience with people pretending to be something they weren't.

"Where does she live?" he continued.

"She's a fellow Texan," Amaya said, realizing how that sounded in the context of what Keith had just mentioned.

Could Loralee be that deceitful?

∼

KEITH DIDN'T like the sound of Loralee Bedder. Was she even female? The profile picture could literally be copied from the internet. The person behind the façade could literally be anyone. It was the exact reason he didn't use those dating apps. Too easy to get burned and he didn't like wasting time or energy.

Even to himself right then, he sounded well beyond his twenty-five years. It wasn't like he didn't take chances. Hell, tracking poachers was one of the most dangerous jobs for a cattle rancher. When it came to his time off work, he was protective.

He pulled up the notes app on his phone and put together a short list of folks he wanted to talk to in person. Loralee, Killian, Marcus the best friend. He also needed to dig into Puddin' Pop's true identity, so he added her name to the bottom of the list. "Sending a message to Loralee might not be the best tact right now. News of the attempt on your life might already be out. If she's innocent, hearing that you want to stop by her home might freak her out and scare her off. If she's guilty, the situation only gets worse from there."

"Should I log onto my account at this point?" Amaya asked.

"How secure is it?"

"Your guess is as good as mine," she said. "I'd say very secure but Dallas PD, lot of help they were, told me not to go on my site for a few days. Honestly, the threats might just freak me out even more. Going out there, posting something might just make the person behind this madder."

"So this murderer just gets to hide behind his or her screen?" he asked with disgust.

"That was my first question to law enforcement," she stated.

"Did they take you seriously?"

"An officer took down my complaint and my information," she said. "But Dallas is a big city and budgets for law enforcement have been cut, as you already know. I'm fine and the threat was pointed directly at me. The detective assigned to my case believes this could blow over if I lay low for a while. Said he would look into it but without a weapon or any idea who might be behind this, he said an investigation would take time. I also saw the bags underneath his eyes, the stubble on his chin, and the rolled-up sleeves in a white button-down shirt that looked like he'd slept in for the past week. He had a roll of TUMS on his desk. Every fifteen minutes like clockwork he peeled one off and then tossed it inside his mouth. Bloodshot eyes from staring at a screen too long told me how overworked he is."

"Did you mention any of this to him?" Keith asked.

KEITH: Firebrand Cowboys 47

"I told him to blink every few minutes when he sat in front of the computer," she said honestly. "Then, I thanked him for his time."

"That scenario doesn't exactly breed a whole lot of confidence in the legal system," Keith pointed out.

"There's a lot going on," she reminded him. He also realized in this conversation how much he loved the sanctity of living on Firebrand land. The peace and quiet. Most of the time, at least.

"Understood," he finally agreed. It was the reason he didn't seek out the news or spend more time than necessary on the internet. The way he saw it, he was better off for it. Growing up a Firebrand, everyone in town made it their business to gossip about his family. He saw no point in putting more of his life on display through social media.

"You might be the first person I've met in a long time that doesn't use social media," Amaya said.

"I'm sure it has its uses," he said. "But it's not for everyone."

It was probably a good thing he'd never heard of Amaya before today anyway, he thought. This way, he didn't see her as some internet sensation on the verge of a breakthrough in her career. He saw her as a real person, sitting here in the flesh. She was a businesswoman who seemed to be savvy. He wasn't surprised she was blowing up online. But he intended to get to the bottom of who was trying to stop her. "I might have a guy who can trace Loralee and come up with a physical address."

Keith fired off a text to Simon, who was the closest thing to a tech genius as anyone Keith had ever known. The two had gone to the same high school until Simon was pulled out for it being too easy. Simon had a knack for programming and other math pursuits. He ended up graduating high school two years early before heading to the University of Texas at Austin, where he would have graduated in three years with honors. The problem was the pressure got to Simon, so he dropped out of school, worked at a coffee shop in downtown Austin and was basically a hacker for hire. It was his way of middle-fingering the system that tried to chew him up and spit him out years before he was mature enough to handle it.

Simon might or might not respond, depending on his mood. Not two seconds after Keith sent the text did the three little dots show up on the screen, a good sign.

Should I ask why you need to find this person?

Keith responded by saying it might be better not to ask questions at the moment, but that he wasn't engaged in illegal activity if that was Simon's true concern. Turned out, Simon wasn't. They settled on a price for the work and then Simon said to hold tight because this shouldn't take long.

When Keith finished texting, he set the phone down in the space between him and Amaya. This wasn't the time to notice her clean floral scent that was like breathing in a spring morning after a good rain or how much it was waking up his senses. He didn't want to—no, couldn't afford to—let an attraction run wild.

"My guy is on it," Keith said.

"What do we do now?"

"We wait for a response," Keith said. His phone dinged as though punctuating his sentence. "That should be my guy now."

"That was fast," Amaya said, amazed.

Keith picked up the cell, impressed by Simon more so than usual. But this also could mean their first real break was coming. He needed to buckle up because he had a feeling this ride was about to get dangerous.

6

Amaya picked up the empty coffee mug on the table beside them, needing to do something with her hands as Keith checked the screen on his phone.

"We have an address," Keith said with enthusiasm. His forehead wrinkled as he kept reading. "Hold on. It's to a library in Houston."

"Does that mean it's fake?" Amaya asked.

"Not necessarily," Keith pondered. "It's possible Loralee is using the public library internet."

"Wouldn't she need ID for that?" Amaya asked before it clicked. "Oh. Never mind. She would use her real name for the library card but not for internet use."

"Those computers are probably set up so they don't collect information about users," Keith surmised, which also made sense. A public computer would most likely warn folks about the dangers of putting their banking and other sensitive information into a shared system. At least she hoped they would. Stealing identities was running rampant as were phishing schemes. Any chance to defraud people and take their money or sell their information was being exploited.

"So, what do we do?" she asked.

"We can go to the library and wait to see if she shows up."

"Except that I don't exactly know what she looks like," Amaya pointed out.

"No," he agreed. "Have you spoken on the phone?"

She shook her head. "Everything is done online. My career was blowing up, and I didn't exactly have time to dot every i or cross every t." She issued a sharp sigh. "I should have been more careful but I didn't see anything like this coming."

"You're an honest person," he pointed out.

"Yes, but I grew up around people trying to take from me and anyone else they could scam," she admitted, beyond frustrated with herself. "I usually know to look out for people on the take. Why didn't I see this coming?"

"It might not be her," he said.

"You should see the text she sent me," Amaya said, cringing at remembering the heated words. "She called me just about every name in the book for reneging on our deal for her to get paid. She blew up at me for being a fraud."

"Do you remember way back in grade school when you're sitting in class and suddenly a stink fills the air?" he asked.

She cocked an eyebrow curious as to where this was heading. "Yes. Why?"

"You see noses wrinkling, but no one speaks up until one person points the finger at someone else," he continued.

It dawned on her what he was about to say. "The smeller is the feller, right? Are you talking about that old saying?"

"That's exactly what I'm referring to," he confirmed. "It became ingrained in middle school culture for a reason."

"Because it's usually true," she said.

He nodded. "Which is why Loralee is at the top of my to-question list."

"Makes sense." She didn't want to think she could have been in a partnership with someone who would try to physically harm her, which brought up an interesting question. "How would Loralee benefit from me dying, though?"

"She might be bidding for your sponsorship," he suggested. "People do all kinds of things to gain advantage in business."

"They'd have to be pretty twisted to want to drug someone in order to abduct them." Her words had the effect of a sucker punch to Keith based on his expression and the way he sucked in a breath. "Did I say something wrong?"

He shook his head.

"Hey, come on," she urged. "I've told you so much about me. Like, I never talk about my family or my past. So, it's not fair for you to zip your mouth closed when I ask a question after stepping on a landmine. That's what I did, wasn't it? Said something that triggered you."

Slowly, he nodded. He chewed on the inside of his jaw. She'd noticed him doing that earlier when he was in deep thought.

"First of all, we'll head to the Houston library if you promise to try to rest for a couple of hours," he wagered.

"Does this mean you'll open up and share why my words a minute ago seemed to knock your breath out?"

"Yes," he said. "But, like you, I don't go around talking about my family problems."

"Oh," she said, realizing the man might have a wife and kid out there somewhere. Her gaze immediately dropped to his ring finger. No band. No tan line. Did this mean he wasn't married? "Do you and your wife have kids?"

Keith shot her a confused look. "I don't have either one." And then it dawned on him. "I was referring to my siblings, cousins, and parents."

"I know all about having a messed up family, Keith. You don't have to shy away from talking to me about yours. Believe me when I say nothing can shock me after finding out my mother was a stripper."

"Oh, I can beat that," he said with resignation.

She rolled up her sleeves and waited.

"How about finding out your mother attempted murder to get a bigger piece of everyone's inheritance?"

"Holy hell," she said before she could reel the words in. The shock was real. "I'm so sorry. You're such a nice guy. It's hard to believe you came from anything other than a loving two-parent family."

"I'd take one decent parent," he said. "But that wasn't in the cards either."

Turned out they had more in common than Amaya realized. Kindred spirits? Was that the reason it was so easy to open up to Keith? "You don't have to say anything else if you don't want to." She, of all people, knew how hard it was to open up about a screwed-up family life. Especially when she worked so hard to put hers behind her.

"It's okay," he said. "You're right. You opened up to me and I owe you the same courtesy. This doesn't have to be a one-way street."

Amaya offered a smile. She reached over and touched his hand, surprised when electricity with the force of a lightning bolt struck with contact. Keith had it all. Intelligence. Good looks. Smokin' hot bod. Kindness. She could tell there was a sense of humor tucked away in there too.

KEITH: Firebrand Cowboys

"Alright. Tell me as much or as little as you want. I'm here to listen."

She leaned against him, shoulder-to-shoulder. Contact might be electric but it also had a calming effect on her.

"Are you sure you can handle this?" Keith asked.

"Remember that part where I told you my mother was a stripper?"

"Yes," he said.

"I can handle anything you can throw at me," she reassured.

∼

KEITH HADN'T UTTERED a word about his mother to anyone outside of the family. With his siblings and cousins, he only listened to what was absolutely necessary, never once speaking up. He took in a deep breath. *Here goes.* "You might be one of the few folks in Texas who doesn't know the last name Firebrand. It's refreshing, actually, so I didn't fill you in. Suffice it to say we're one of the most, if not *the* most, successful cattle ranching families in the state."

"Whoa. That sounds big."

Amaya's shoulder against his, their connection, gave him courage to keep talking.

"It is," he admitted.

"Are you rich?"

The innocent question made him laugh. "You could say that."

"Whoa."

"You already said that," he teased, appreciating the break in tension.

"Sorry. You don't come across as wealthy. You're too down-to-earth."

"It's the ranching blood in me," he said. "There's something about working cattle, being out on the land, that keeps you grounded. Except for my mother, of course. My grandfather was a cranky old bastard. He created a competitive environment between his two sons, my father and uncle. They pretty much hated each other growing up. Each one constantly trying to outdo the other. Neither were good humans, which probably should have been the real goal. But my grandfather wasn't having it. He believed competition bred winners, and he wanted a winner taking the proverbial reigns to the business he built from scratch."

"Sounds intense," Amaya offered.

The breath he blew out made a fsh-type noise. "It was… is… I've been thinking a lot about his legacy lately, but that's a whole different story."

"One I'd like to hear at some point," Amaya said. Did she realize how soothing her voice was? Or that every time she spoke it was like balm to a broken soul?

"My mother decided she wanted more of the wealth, once she realized my grandfather wasn't going to be around much longer, given his advanced age," Keith explained. "She got wind of him giving money to someone he cared a great deal about so she attempted m…" Could he say the word out loud? Keith steeled his nerves and bowed his head. Not speaking it didn't make it any less true. "She tried to take someone's life."

"I'm so sorry," Amaya soothed. The next thing he knew, her arm looped around his midsection. There was no judgment in her voice, which was also foreign to him. Folks in his hometown seemed to have made a sport out of judging his side of the family tree. His parents' actions had added fuel to the fire. His mother had always been over the top, showing off their money with expensive clothes. She was always dressed to the nines with hair and make-up done up. She gave the town plenty of reasons to talk behind her back, and her children suffered because of it.

"Now, she's in jail in Houston, after being moved from Lone Star Pass, because she was severely beaten in the county jail," he added.

"That's not right," Amaya defended. "She should be held safely while waiting for her trial date." She, of all people, would understand the pain of having a family member locked behind bars. Guilty or not, it didn't matter. Having someone you cared about locked in jail with other folks who decided to meter out their own justice was the worst feeling.

"At least the lawyer was able to get her moved to a bigger city where she has a chance at a fair trial," he said.

"I'm sorry for all that you're going through," she said. "You didn't ask for any of this and it's not fair."

"It's life, right?" was all he could say. No one was immune to having their world turned upside-down on a dime. Not him. Not other rich folks. Not poor people. Life didn't discriminate; It handed out crappy hands to everyone equally. And, hopefully, it balanced with sending goodness too. Though that was never guaranteed.

"I know," she said. "But that doesn't mean it sucks any less."

"Those words mean a lot." Talking about his mother and their family situation wasn't as awful as he'd been afraid it might be. Mostly, he did anything and everything to distract himself from the drama, which also included ignoring it altogether. Still, there was always an elephant in the room. "You're easy to talk to."

"We just have common ground when it comes to our families," she clarified. "But can I ask you a question?"

He readied himself for the worst. "Go for it."

"Why are you starting a business if you come from a rich family?" She tensed ever so slightly like she was preparing for a punch. Did she expect him to become defensive? Fly off the handle?

Damn.

"It's important to strike out on my own and not rely on family funds to make a living," he said. "I need independence and not an inheritance handed to me by birthright."

"You work the ranch, right?"

"Yes," he confirmed.

"Have you worked the ranch your entire life?" she asked.

"Yes."

"And it wouldn't work the same or run as efficiently without you and the others working the cattle and the operation," she said. "And I right about that?"

"You nailed it," he said on a chuckle. He was starting to see where she was headed with all this. "The place wouldn't be the same. One of us or a few of us can be gone throughout the year, but the operation runs most efficiently when we're all there with all hands on deck."

"Running a business is hard work," she said. "Believe me. I know. Everyone talks about being able to set their own hours when they own their own business. The truth for most is you'll work all hours of the day and night while you're trying to get off the ground. Possibly even more as your business grows." She paused a few beats. "How old are you?"

"Twenty-five."

She leaned back. "I'd say that you've been integral in the success of Firebrand Ranch, or whatever the name is, and the operation wouldn't be nearly where it is today without your blood, sweat, and tears along with your siblings and cousins. So, basically, you deserve a share in the business.

No one is giving you a handout. In fact, they're lucky to have you at all. And that goes for your relatives too. Otherwise, it's child labor from your youth and that would be illegal. You've put in the time and deserve the rewards."

Keith couldn't hold a smile back. "I've never really thought about it like that. But you're making a lot of sense."

He could easily see how successful a businesswoman Amaya would be. It was no wonder she'd built a successful business.

"You're welcome," she said with a self-satisfied grin. Those pink lips called to him. It was taking all his willpower not to ask permission to kiss them. "And no charge for the advice. This one is between friends."

Friends?

An urge to be a whole lot more welled up inside Keith. He quashed it as best as he could, reminding himself it would be unprofessional to kiss a client, no matter how strong the pull between them. Or how tempting she might be. Or how rare and elusive a feeling like this was.

Shame.

7

Satisfied with her persuasive skills, Amaya folded her arms across her chest and leaned back.

"By your logic, I should probably get the smallest share, since I'm the youngest on my side of the family then," Keith mused.

"Untrue," Amaya countered.

"How do you figure?" he asked, mirroring her body language. "I've been around to help build the business less time than the others."

"Sure," she agreed. "However, you'll be around long after they are gone, so they're hedging their bets on you for the future of the ranch."

Keith laughed and it was the best sound. It filled the room with warmth.

"Ever consider becoming a lawyer?" he teased.

"Too much boring reading," she quipped with a smile that cut straight to his heart.

He dropped his hands to his knees and his face morphed to a more serious look. "Tell me honestly. Do you need sleep?"

Behind her, the sun was already peeking through buildings. "I couldn't if I tried." It was easy to tell when she could barely hold her eyes open anymore. Yawning gave her away. It wasn't subtle. "Do you need to grab a few hours? Because I can figure out something to do in the meantime."

"Nah, I'm good," he reassured.

"I could use food, though," she said.

Keith stood and walked over to the coffee machine area. He produced a room service menu. "Take a look and see if anything suits you."

"Okay, but you have to let me pay you back for all this," she insisted. "I know you're working for free right now and it's not fair of me to run up the bill."

Keith waved a hand like it was no big deal. "Now that we're friends, I'd do for you even if you weren't my first client." He chuckled that low rumble. "Do me a favor and order something hearty for me while I grab a quick shower."

Amaya didn't want the image of a naked Keith Firebrand burned into her thoughts but there it was just the same. She shook her head like she could shake it out as he grabbed a backpack and then headed for the master bath. She could use a shower after she ate. At least she's changed into something comfortable. He'd stayed in jeans and boots. Jeans that had looked a little too good hung low on his hips. He had the kind of body that formed an improbably V. All lean muscles. He was strong too. Those muscles weren't just for show.

She perused the menu, which was fancier than she realized it would be. There was an omelet, bacon, and toast item that she thought Keith might like. It was basically taking a stab in the dark, since they'd never shared a meal before and she had no idea what his habits were. He'd asked for something substantial, though. On top of the omelet, she ordered eggs benedict. The slice of ham along with the eggs would be good protein for him. That came with a side of hash browns and three pancakes.

Even though there was a coffee machine in the room, she ordered a fresh carafe. If they were at her apartment, she would whip up a cup using her French Press and coffee grounds from Central Market. She was presently into a Jamaican bean. She was a halfway decent cook thanks to having to fend for herself most of her life.

The shower water came on in the next room. She closed her eyes and tried to blank out the sexy image. What could she say? Keith was perfection. She could only imagine how perfect his body would be naked.

Clearly, Amaya was more tired than she realized. Could she please stop obsessing over the ridiculously hot guy in the shower? This was his first security gig and they were making headway on figuring out who was trying to erase her from the planet.

That was it. That was the reason she was focusing on him. Otherwise, she felt too out of control.

Good to know. At least she'd solved one problem for the day. Refocusing on the menu, she walked over to the phone on the desk. It had been a long time since she'd gone anywhere or stayed in a hotel, so having a landline was a throwback to a time before she could remember. She picked up the receiver and hit the button for room service.

The person on the other end had a calming voice when he answered, calling Keith by his last name. She was taken back at the lack of privacy, but then her generation had no misgivings they actually would have it, so this shouldn't catch her off guard. Plus, this hotel was the most expensive in Austin. There'd been no check-in line. The person behind the counter had been nothing but kind. She believed she saw a hint of recognition in the check-in clerk's eyes when she looked up from her screen at Keith. Amaya had chalked up the reaction to his good looks but, no, she must have recognized a Firebrand when she saw one.

Had he been here before? Or was she one of the only people in Texas who didn't automatically know who he was?

Rather than give her name or correct the phone attendant, Amaya gave the order and then hung up the phone. She thought about the kind of money Keith must have to be able to afford a place like this. He hadn't batted an eyelash as he plunked his credit card down. She'd hung back so the clerk couldn't get a good look at her. Funnily enough, she'd worried about being the one who was recognized, especially when he was the one to pay for the room.

This room wasn't exactly basic. A suite in a hotel like this one must cost...what? A thousand a night? Fifteen hundred? It was a good thing they were getting the hell out of there before she ran up a bill she couldn't afford to repay. Now that she understood the situation, there was no way she was allowing Keith to shoulder the cost of the room, especially when she'd been the one to insist on the first-class accommodations. Now that she knew he was loaded, she really didn't want to take advantage of his generosity.

Besides, she was getting to know Keith. He was a good person who would offer a hand to anyone in need.

The spigot shut off in the next room. The order taker on the phone had said food would be sent up in the next twenty to thirty minutes. Five minutes had passed since making the order. If Amaya hurried, she had time to take a shower before the food arrived.

Keith emerged wearing a fresh pair of jeans and no shirt. A towel was wrapped around the back of his neck. Amaya forced her gaze away from the droplets of water rolling down his pectorals.

"Mind if I grab a shower?" she asked, staring at the carpet.

"Go ahead," he responded.

"The food is ordered and should be here in fifteen to twenty minutes," she said. "I won't take long."

"There's a robe hanging on the back of the door in case you need to throw it on to eat," he offered. His voice cracked. Was he having some of the same thoughts she was having?

A smile tugged at the corners of her lips thinking she might be having the same effect on him. There was a modicum of enjoyment to be had in the knowledge. Before she got too tickled with herself, she picked up her overnight bag and headed toward the bathroom.

~

ON THE HOUSTON TRIP, Keith needed to work in a visit to see his mother. He pulled up the map feature on his phone. The downtown Houston public library was on McKinney Street across from Houston City Hall and Hermann Square.

It would be easy enough to blend in a busy area. One that had pedestrian traffic. Most folks didn't walk around in Texas, unless he counted Austin with its overabundance of university students without transportation. Folks were out all times of the day and night there, filling the sidewalks. The aerial view looked much like an ant farm from his childhood anywhere near the university. Most complained about the heat in the Lone Star State, but college students didn't seem to mind.

Considering UT was long considered a top-party school,

he figured half the young people were probably too buzzed to notice the weather.

A knock sounded at the door as he studied the map. A thought niggled at the back of his mind but he couldn't quite reach it as he instinctively headed to the door of the suite. The prickly feeling causing the tiny hairs on the back of his neck to stand up stopped him halfway across the room.

He diverted course to his backpack where he kept a Sig Sauer, a small handgun that was easy to conceal and just as deadly as the rest.

After retrieving the weapon, he jogged over to the door and risked a glance through the peephole. White covered the hole. A napkin? "Can I help you?"

"Room service," an unfamiliar male voice said. The man on the other side of the door turned his face to the peephole and smiled.

Nope. Keith didn't recognize him. Did room service attendants really wear chef hats? Because this one did. He stepped aside to reveal a tray full of silver domes and a carafe of coffee with all the trimmings to go with it.

It paid to be paranoid in Keith's new line of work, hell in life, but pulling a gun on a room service attendant was overkill.

Keith opened the door a crack, trying to hide the fact he was holding a gun. "You can leave the cart right there. I'll take it from here." He exposed just enough of his upper body for the young blue-eyed guy to see he wasn't decent.

"Okay, no problem, Mr. Firebrand," Blue Eyes said. "If I could get you to sign the ticket, I'll be on my way."

More warning bells sounded in the back of Keith's mind, but he wrote them off as being paranoid. The cart was filled with food and drinks. Blue Eyes was young and wearing full catering garb.

Was that the part that bothered Keith?

The attendant's look was overkill. He picked up a black leather folder, no doubt holding the ticket inside, and reached his hand inside the door. Keith took the offering as he placed his bare foot against the door to ensure it didn't open an inch more.

Blue Eyes seemed taken back as he held his ground. He also looked keenly aware that Keith wasn't going to tolerate any funny business. If Blue Eyes was sizing Keith up, he wasn't going to get far.

"Is there a lady inside the room, sir?" Blue Eyes asked.

"My girlfriend called the order in," Keith lied. He didn't like deception, especially after everything his family had been through, but he was playing a role here and he didn't like the fact Blue Eyes was asking about Amaya. "Why?"

"Oh, nothing, sorry to ask, but..." Blue Eyes registered a small smile, looking younger than his early twenty-ish years. He also looked dodgy like he had something to say but wasn't sure if he should come out with it.

"Something on your mind?" Keith asked, figuring he could prod the young man into answering.

Blue Eyes checked left and then right. "There's a rumor going around the hotel Amaya Katz is staying with us."

Keith was certain this guy was breaking protocol in asking about a guest. He also realized she was more visible than he'd estimated. Staying here much longer was a mistake. Word traveled fast with phones and internet accessible twenty-four hours a day, seven days a week. He probably shouldn't be too surprised she'd been recognized by the staff. She was, after all, from Texas.

"Is that true?" Blue Eyes asked. His face turned six shades of red.

"No, sorry," Keith said. "My girlfriend's name is Lisa." He pulled the first name that came to mind.

"Do me a favor," Blue Eyes said, leaning in. "Please don't tell my manager that I asked. I'd get fired."

"I won't," Keith promised. "But I'd think twice before giving into or starting rumors about your guests. People come here for privacy, not to be stalked by employees who should be back in the kitchen ready to deliver the next order."

"Yes, sir."

Blue Eyes saluted before disappearing. He left without getting the signature but Keith could leave it in the room. He didn't like the paperwork trail he was leaving behind though. It had been a snap decision to come here to appease Amaya.

A mistake?

He grabbed the cart, figuring they had time to get a meal in them along with a fresh cup of coffee, before hitting the road to Houston. The trip wouldn't take more than three hours if they managed to avoid the traffic. But then, rush hour in Austin started early and ended late. Some said it was twenty-four hours a day but there'd been some reprieve since they'd built the loop. Much like other growing metropolitan areas in Texas, roads couldn't keep up with the influx of vehicles.

With the fluffy white bathrobe pulled up to her neck, Amaya joined him. "My stomach growled the minute I smelled this. It must be amazing." She took in a deep breath.

"We should probably eat fast," he warned as he rolled the office chair toward her so she could sit down and eat.

"Okay," she said, drawing out the word. "What did I miss?"

"Word is out that you're staying at the hotel," he stated as he started taking metal domes off plates of food. He poured two cups of black coffee as Amaya helped set the table, unrolling the silverware from white napkins.

"That's no good," she said.

"My thoughts exactly."

"What makes you say that, though?" she asked as she took the seat and then started digging in.

"The room service attendant specifically asked about you." He dug into the omelet Amaya had signaled was his plate. "It's probably a good idea to try to disguise you on the way out."

As a statuesque, caramel-toned skin, exceedingly beautiful woman, they had their work cut out for them.

"I sure as hell hope Houston has answers," she said. "Hiding in plain sight might not have been my best suggestion."

"We can't anticipate every possible issue," he said. Moving forward, though, he would be smarter about not allowing her to be seen.

He would figure out a way to find Loralee Bedder despite the fact they would be searching for a needle in a haystack.

Resting all his hopes on Houston might not be a great plan but it was the only one he had. He had a bad feeling about visiting the library.

8

Amaya polished off her plate fast. Probably too fast. She would most likely pay for the move with indigestion. But that was future Amaya's problem. Right now Amaya had to get something in her stomach so they could get the hell out of the hotel before word spread. Between cell phones and the internet, word could spread like wildfire in a drought.

The coffee burned her lips so she grabbed a couple of ice cubes from her water and stirred them in. The temperature lowered enough for her to take a couple of big swigs, before racing into the bedroom to get dressed.

She probably should have been embarrassed to be wearing only a robe a few minutes ago, except that she didn't feel self-conscious at all being near Keith. He had a calming effect on her that was unusual considering he also caused her stomach to flip-flop when he was near. It was a strange effect but addictive. And she knew where addictions landed a person. In her childhood, she'd seen enough to last a lifetime.

Within seven minutes, Amaya was dressed and had

freshened up her face along with fixing her hair. She was good to go.

Walking into the living room, an image stopped her cold. Keith stood at the door, eyeing the peephole. The glint of metal drew her gaze. He was holding a gun behind his back. "What is it? What's going on?"

"A crowd is gathering," he said with a muttered curse. "We shouldn't have waited to get the hell out of here."

"Leaving incognito doesn't seem to be an option now," she reasoned as an idea popped. "If you can't beat 'em, join 'em."

"What? No." His tone was defensive and finite but he wasn't seeing the big picture yet.

"You'll see," she reassured. "Finish getting dressed and we'll walk right out the door. Folks will most likely have their cameras out."

"Which is exactly what I'm trying to avoid."

"We can't, so we have to embrace it instead," she reasoned. "Plus, it'll have the added benefit of making everyone believe I'm in Austin. People will figure me out eventually in Houston too, but once we're in the clear I can change my appearance."

"You look like a model," he pointed out. "There's no one out there as beautiful, striking, or memorable as you."

The compliment caused her cheeks to flush, so she was relieved his gaze was fixed on the activity in the hallway and not her. He didn't mean it in the way she wanted him to anyway. Seeing her reaction would give away her attraction to the man, an attraction she wanted to keep to herself at present because it wasn't going anywhere. He might have felt reciprocation, but that didn't mean anything could come of it. Not only did they lead separate lives but they were very different people.

KEITH: Firebrand Cowboys 69

She would leave it at that.

"The proverbial cat is out of the bag, Keith. In my experience, it's time to own it," she finally said when he turned to look at her. "Trust me?"

He bit down on his bottom lip before offering a slight nod. His trust was tentative but she'd take it.

"Okay, then," she said with a new sense of confidence. "Get dressed."

He didn't leave the room. Instead he grabbed his backpack and then grabbed a long-sleeve pullover. She kept her eyes forward with him in the peripheral, so she wouldn't gawk at the man's perfect bod. What could she say? He stirred an attraction in her that reached deep in her core. Keith Firebrand was a dangerous distraction.

Refocusing, she grabbed her purse and put on rebel red lipstick. She gathered her things and placed them inside her overnight bag.

"Ready?" she asked as Keith shouldered his backpack.

"As much as I'll ever be," he confided. A guy like him would shun the spotlight. He was one of the most low-key guys she'd ever been around. Was his family the center of attention in his hometown?

Amaya had craved the attention from her channel until it turned ugly. Even so, she would ride this out and then pick up the pieces. Quitting wasn't an option. All she needed was to regroup and come up with another plan to revive her business. Or start a new one. She could come up with a new concept. Killian had wanted to be an influencer. Marky had been asking questions about how to get started.

Maybe she could move behind the scenes to help one of them for a piece of the action?

"I'll go out first," she said. "Hopefully, that way no one will pay much attention to you while you snag an elevator."

"We don't know who is out there, Amaya."

"I realize that," she said with a frown. "But it's only going to get worse out there the longer we wait."

"Not if we call the law," he surmised.

"I doubt they'll be able to do much," she said. "They haven't exactly been helpful so far. With all that's going on in their world, they have bigger fish to fry than helping me."

"We don't know that," he said.

What sounded like a battering ram slammed into the door.

"We have to go now," Amaya urged. "Before this gets worse."

Amaya opened the door and walked straight into the small crowd. She didn't hold the door open for Keith or wait for him, figuring it was his best chance to slip out behind her. People could be unpredictable. Her reputation as an influencer had been damaged thanks to an unidentified person.

Four tweens practically assaulted her. Their faces lit up and they gave out a little squeal of excitement, which she took as a good sign this group was friendly. The group backed her up against a plant as she eased their backs toward the door she'd just exited.

Keith slipped past without anyone giving him a second look. She, however, was trapped. Even if he could bring the car around without drawing attention, she might not be able to unpin herself from this plant and wall.

"Would you sign this, please?" a small voice asked.

Amaya turned to her right to see the sweetest smiling face beaming up at her. The girl couldn't be more than eleven or twelve years old. At that moment, it struck her being an influencer was more than just peddling a corporation's product to get the most money. Those big, adoring hazel eyes deserved more from Amaya than essentially selling her followers to the highest bidder.

She bit back a curse as she smiled at the girl and took the printed picture to sign in.

"I don't have a pen," the girl meekly said.

"Anyone?" Amaya looked over the heads to see if anyone had a marker.

"Here you go," a voice said. The voice caused a chill to race down her back. What was her father doing here?

Since a family reunion wasn't high on her list, she edged away from him and deeper into the group to her right after taking the black marker.

The man, her father, was wearing a Dallas Cowboys ball cap. Didn't he realize he was mixing his sports? A baseball cap should have the Rangers on it, not a football team. It irritated her.

The Cowboys ball cap shifted directions every time she did, like a shark tracking prey. It was making its way toward her as she kept one eye on the silver Star logo.

The elevator dinged and the door opened. There was no way she would be able to make it to Keith as more joined the crowd until claustrophobia made the walls feel like they were starting to close in. Her shirt suddenly felt like it shrank four sizes. Breathing caused pain in her chest.

Despite being taller than most everyone there, she'd lost visual with Keith.

Panic gripped her.

∼

THE ELEVATOR DOORS CLOSED. Keith refused to get on without Amaya. Just as he was about to shout to her, a voice cut through the buzz of the small crowd.

"Everyone, step aside," the room service attendant from a few minutes ago ordered. He had a surprising note of authority.

Keith pressed the button again to reopen the doors but the elevator was already on its way down. Dammit. He'd lost valuable seconds by not standing inside and holding it. He pressed the button a couple more times as the crowd split like the Red Sea at Moses' command.

Blue Eyes walked straight up to Amaya and took her arm. "This way." He waved his free hand. "Everyone back to your rooms before I call security."

A reluctant crowd dispersed, save for a man wearing a Dallas Cowboys baseball cap, the brim low enough to hide a good portion of his face as he tucked his chin to chest. He hesitated for a few seconds, looking like he might make a move for Amaya. An ominous feeling settled over Keith and those tiny hairs on the back of his neck pricked again. Had he been lurking in the hall earlier?

Keith jumped into action, coming up behind the man and grabbing his right arm. He jacked the man's arm behind his back, causing him to release an audible grunt. "Not today sonofabitch."

He watched as Blue Eyes maneuvered Amaya through the dispersing crowd.

"Let go or I'll press charges," the man said. Technically, he wasn't doing anything wrong other than crowding the hallway in front of Amaya's hotel room door. It wasn't against the law, so the man had a point.

Keith released Cowboy Cap's arm. The man fled without so much as turning around to get a good look at Keith. Had he written Keith off as security, a hired hand? Therefore, didn't need a close-up?

The mystery guy was older, somewhere in middle age

from what Keith could tell. Caucasian. The man had tanned, leathery skin that said he spent a decent amount of time in the sun. His frame was tall but he was built more like a runner than a bodybuilder. The fact his hands were manicured instead of rough said he didn't get the tan from doing work outside. He had more of a poolside tan. The kind someone got from intentionally laying out in the sun rather than the one most ranchers had, which concentrated tan marks on the neck and arms.

Keith had always been good about wearing gloves and long sleeves along with a cowboy hat that provided coverage when he worked fences. He knew enough about sun damage to throw on sunblock before he headed outside in the unrelenting Texas sun during summer months. It got so hot the pavement literally melted the rubber on the soles of his shoes.

He took note of Cowboy Cap, and then moved toward Amaya and Blue Eyes. The crowd was gone, which made it easy to follow the pair. Blue Eyes led her down the hallway and to a door he had to badge into. Keith caught up to them before the door closed and slipped inside.

"Hey," Blue Eyes said protectively, as he turned to scold Keith. He realized who had followed and clamped his mouth shut.

"Keith," Amaya said as she turned around. The door clicked closed as she threw her arms around his neck and buried her face in his chest.

"You're safe now," Keith reassured.

"I got so claustrophobic," she said. "That's never happened to me before. I panicked and just kept trying to inch away to find more space. Space that wasn't there. I couldn't see you and all I could think was that something would separate us."

"I'm here," he whispered into her ear. "I'm not going anywhere. You have my word."

He looped his arms around her waist as she pressed her body flush against his.

Keith ignored the sudden ache in his chest to be alone with her. As much as he wanted to stay rooted to this exact spot until her heart stopped thundering, they needed to move if he was going to make good on his promise to keep her safe.

He made eye contact with Blue Eyes, who gave a pleading look. Keith nodded before taking Amaya's hand. He'd felt her body tremble against his, which had sent anger coursing through his veins.

"Let's get to my truck," he said, catching her gaze and holding onto it. He could stare into those honey-browns of hers until the cows came home. But this wasn't the time to get lost in her soulful eyes.

Blue Eyes led them through a labyrinth of back hallways. The plush carpet had ended the minute they'd stepped onto the side the worker had had to use his badge to access. This was the vein of the hotel operation, pumping life-giving blood to various areas of the building. This was where the real work was done, hoofing it to bring pampered guests whatever they could dream up.

Keith could only imagine what that might be. His own mother had taken shopping trips to Houston, no doubt staying in a hotel like one of these. He could envision his mother ordering room service, in-room spa services, and generally living it up. Drinking her champagne. Was Houston where she'd plotted murder?

His memories of her would forever be tainted. They weren't all that good to begin with. She wasn't exactly the kind of mother who baked cookies or cooked dinners. She wasn't a nurturer; there were no goodnight hugs or tucking anyone in bed. She didn't show up to teacher conferences or athletic events, no matter how many sports he played. His mother wasn't singling him out to cold-shoulder either. She hadn't gone to any events for any one of her nine sons. Keith would never understand why the woman had to have so many children in the first place, considering she couldn't be bothered with them. Even when they were little, she'd hired someone else to take care of them.

Keith had the least amount of memories of his parents. Maybe because he'd shown up last. His brother had shown him the ropes. He'd been close with a couple of his cousins at one point in time.

The time before life spun out of control and division lines were drawn. His oldest brother and cousin had never been close. The other side of the family had been making an effort to mend fences even after Keith's mother had attempted murder to snatch more of the inheritance.

And now his mother's actions could destroy the Firebrands forever.

9

In those few moments of panic when Amaya had lost sight of Keith, she'd been struck by how much she'd come to depend on him in such a short amount of time. Trust wasn't something she handed out easily.

There was something about Keith that made her feel like she'd known him for years, rather than hours. Old soul? Kindred spirit?

Either way, she tightened her grip around his hand as they followed the hotel worker with pale blue eyes.

"This door leads to the garage where your vehicle would have been parked," the worker wearing a white chef's hat said. "I can retrieve the keys if you want."

"I always keep a spare," Keith said, motioning toward his backpack. "We'll be fine."

"Okay then, I should get back to work."

"Do you mind using a courier to deliver my other key back to Firebrand Ranch?" Keith asked.

"I know who you are, sir," the worker said with a smile. "And it would be my pleasure to take care of it."

"Put the expense on my card," Keith instructed. He let go

of Amaya's hand long enough to pull a wad of clipped money out of the side pocket of his backpack. He peeled off a couple of hundred-dollar bills and then shook the worker's hand, placing the money in his palm.

"Thank you, sir," the worker said with ease. It was like this kind of thing happened on a regular basis, whereas Amaya was completely out of her league despite her recent success. She had only dreamed of having the kind of money that could get her walked down secret hallways and pay off people who would jump through hoops at her command. But even more important to her was the stability it would bring. The steady meals on the dinner table instead of going to be hungry. Money, or lack of it, had caused most of her problems as a child.

Her father was always chasing it, angry that he didn't have it, or claiming he was about to get it. She still remembered the time they had ten dollars to their name and no milk left. Her father had taken the last few dollars from her coin jar. She'd been about eleven years old at the time. Instead of coming home with a gallon of milk, bread, and peanut butter like he was supposed to, he held up a ticket and said he had something better.

It was their ticket out of debt. There'd been a wildness to his eyes that night. She'd been too young to understand it back then. Now, she would have questioned whether or not he was high or drunk.

The ticket, it turned out, was a losing lottery number. But he'd hawked her and Killian up the rest of the evening. He'd jump on the bed with them, holding onto the ticket. At eleven, she believed some external force had sent him the numbers to play. She'd blocked out which one he'd claimed had given him the vision with the right numbers to play.

She'd bought the story hook, line, and sinker. So had Killian.

They'd stayed up long past their bedtime. Drank water instead of the glass of milk they'd been promised before bed. And woke the next morning to their father sitting at the table, drinking his black coffee because there was no milk.

He'd been in a good mood, convinced the ticket was going to pay when the Texas Lotto commissioner pulled the numbers. They'd had to wait until 10:12 that night. Amaya and Killian had spent the day deciding the first thing they were going to buy with their share of the winnings. For Amaya, it was going to be a pony. Impractical. Yes. Did she care at eleven years old? No.

Killian was four years older, barely fifteen. He'd always been young for his age if that made sense. He'd been the class clown during school. Either distracting attention from the fact he struggled to read or from the hand-me-down clothes they'd worn. Now, she had a feeling her brother had an undiagnosed learning disorder. Give him an alarm clock and he could take it apart with no problem. Put it back together too. Hand him a textbook and ask him to read from a page, and he struggled.

He did fine with math unless he was asked to solve a word problem she'd later realized. After a deep dive on the internet, she figured he might be dyslexic without ever knowing it.

After talking to Keith, who apparently had money to spare, Amaya was beginning to realize bucketloads of money might not be the end all, be all. In fact, after learning about his mother, it could make people become even greedier. Having tons of it didn't necessarily mean the stability she craved.

Two minutes after saying goodbye to the hotel worker,

they were inside Keith's truck and he was snaking out of the parking lot. Her mind bounced back to the shock in the Cowboys ball cap.

"My dad was there," she said to Keith after a few moments of silence.

"Was he?" The tone in Keith's voice said he was clicking together the pieces.

"He had on a Cowboys ball cap," she said.

Keith tapped the steering wheel with the palm of his hand. "I grabbed him because his eyes were laser-focused on you. I jacked his hand up his back and told him to walk away. Did I do the wrong thing?"

"No," she said. "In fact, I want to thank you. I have no idea how he knew where I was or even that he'd figured out my new last name. He doesn't have the kind of money to stay in a hotel that nice and I can't imagine anything has changed with his financial situation, so I know he wasn't a guest."

Keith sat quietly. The unspoken accusation sat heavy between them. To Keith's credit, he didn't speak the words out loud but she knew exactly what he was thinking based on his silence.

"I'd like to think he was there altruistically, to reconnect with the daughter he hasn't spoken to in more years than I care to count," she said, her chest deflating. "But my instincts say he showed up to figure out how to get a piece of the pie when I make a comeback. Not that that will ever happen."

At this point, she wasn't certain she ever wanted to step back into the limelight. One minute, she'd been on top of the world. The next, receiving death threats from people who were supposed to be her fans and followers.

When the internet tide turned, it became a tsunami that

flipped a person upside down, disorienting them. She'd be sucked into the wave, churned, beaten to a pulp.

"Give it a few weeks," he said as though he could read her mind, his tone reassuring. "These things blow up all the time and everyone freaks out for a while until the next big thing happens. The tide turns and everyone's attention shifts. People have the attention span of a gnat these days."

"I appreciate you trying to comfort me," she said, wishing it could all be that simple. "But what if it doesn't work that way for me?"

"Then you'll find another way to be successful," he said without hesitation. Why did someone believing in her cause her discomfort? "You're not just smart, you're savvy. You were already growing a business from the ground up with no seed money to speak of. You're here, actively trying to get to the bottom of what's going on."

"What if he's responsible?" she asked, unable to say his name out loud.

Keith shook his head. "You haven't seen him in how long?"

"Years," she admitted.

"Why show up when you're at your weakest point, if all he cared about was trying to get money from you?" he asked.

"I don't know," she said. "But I wouldn't put anything past him. He shows up the sympathetic father and then holds his hand out the minute money starts rolling in again. What if he thinks I'm his lotto ticket?"

The thought was a knife stab to the chest. She hated it. But she wouldn't put it past her father.

∽

THE REST of the almost three-hour drive to Houston flew by. Keith wondered why Amaya's father hadn't identified himself to Keith. But he didn't ask. Amaya was already distraught and it was clear she had the same information as Keith. Neither had answers to the man's behavior, which could only be classified as strange.

Before Keith knew it, he was searching for a parking spot. "I'd rather not run my card, since we've been seen together. I don't want to give away our new location."

Finding free parking downtown was no small feat.

"I don't mind walking," she said, her finger tapping on the armrest. She'd been doing that and staring out the window for the last half hour of the ride. Either deep in thought or barely gripping her frustration, Amaya wasn't the kind to give away how she was feeling. Instead, she developed a laser-like focus and went deep inside her head.

"We might have to," he said as he circled the block for the third time. He caught sight of Legacy Parking at Louisiana and McKinney, and saw little metal boxes for cash. "We might have just hit the jackpot."

They parked. He pulled out a baseball cap and one of his jackets from the backseat of the truck. "Take these and put them on."

Amaya did, but there was no disguising looks like hers. Loralee wouldn't have to look carefully to be able to pick Amaya out of a crowd. But the hats would have to do.

They walked around Wells Fargo Plaza and up Lamar toward the Julia Ideson building. The public library was just up the street from there. At almost ten o'clock in the morning, buildings shaded them from some of the sun exposure. The library opened at nine, so they should be good to go there.

The problem was they didn't know who they were

looking for. He pulled up the photo of Loralee Bedder on his phone and tilted the screen for Amaya to see while they waited to cross the street.

"The more I look at the picture, the more I think it's just a random face," she revealed.

He nodded. "I'd been thinking along the same lines ever since you showed it to me. Isn't that half the draw of the internet? You can be anyone you want. Look like anyone you want. You're the only one who has to know what you really look like."

"It's true."

"How did she come to work for you?" he asked.

"She approached me about a year ago," Amaya explained. "Said she liked what was happening on my channel and that she would like to offer her services to help me grow. I immediately told her that I wasn't hiring, because I was just barely making enough to keep my own lights on. She offered to work for free until I could afford to pay her."

"If she's legit, she must work for others," Keith pointed out.

"It stands to reason she would," Amaya agreed. "This could be how she tried to build her own business. Offer to work for free to several people, and that way she was able to hedge her bets that one of us might come out a winner."

"But she threatened you when the 'so-called truth' about you leaked," he said.

"I took it as her blowing off steam until she disappeared on me," she said. "That's when I started to wonder about her. And then, of course, when I was drugged, that sent my mind reeling. Funny enough, I didn't consider her as a suspect at first."

"Because the two of you had been working together for the past year?"

"I guess," she admitted. "You think you know someone but the truth is that we've never met, never gone out for coffee. We've never had a drink or gone out for tacos. Why would I think that I knew her?"

"The internet has a way of making folks believe they have a lot of friends," he said. "Or so I've heard. It's one of many reasons I can't be bothered." He held up his phone. "If someone wants to get to know me, they're going to have to do it the old-fashioned way."

"How is that working out for you?" she asked.

He chuckled. "Considering I haven't made a new friend in longer than I care to remember, probably not great."

"Internet dating is a whole different ballgame," she admitted.

He was just shooting the breeze, trying to get Amaya to relax. They didn't know who or what they were looking for, but they could ask around the library. "Speaking of which, Loralee, if that's really her name, would have likely been at the library reserving a computer. Someone should be able to identify her if this picture is real or possibly give us a description of their top female users."

"You made a good point earlier, though," she said. "What if Loralee isn't even a woman? What if 'she' is really a man pretending to be a woman? It would lower my guard, wouldn't it? I mean, if you think about it. I might be more suspicious of a guy for volunteering to be my right hand. But a woman? Not so much."

"I guess we need to ask the library staff about anyone who comes in daily to use the computers over the past year," he said. "Have you ever communicated with Loralee outside of business hours? At night? Or early in the morning, like six a.m.?"

"Honestly, I can't remember," she said, exhaling as her

chest deflated a little bit. "The details are a little blurry. I don't recall e-mailing all hours of the night, but she didn't always get back to me right away. I knew she had other clients. Or at least, that was part of her schtick—if it turns out to be one."

"We'll say for argument's sake she only returned e-mails during library hours," he said. "There is the possibility someone is computer savvy enough to ping the library while they're sitting in a random coffee shop somewhere around here or, if they're good enough, they can bounce their signal from just about anywhere."

"Which would mean we're barking up the wrong tree," she said.

"We won't know until we ask around," he pointed out. "Plus, there's the off chance we'll actually run into her this morning. Let's assume the person is actually a woman."

"I could swear she is, but I guess I could be fooled," she admitted. "I think in terms of a grown man sitting behind a computer targeting children who are young and naïve and wouldn't catch any of the perp's slipups. How could someone stay in character long enough to convince someone on the other end?"

She was spinning out and Keith could see frustration rattling her brain.

"If not here, we'll find answers somewhere else," he said. "We won't stop until we do. Okay?"

He reached for her hand and then linked their fingers as she nodded.

"I promise." Even as he said those two words, he realized he might not be able to deliver on his word. And his word was gold.

Stopping, he stared at the modern-looking structure. Maybe they could find answers inside. "I'll ask questions but

I want you to watch for reactions to our presence. Especially anyone who seems too interested in you being there."

Were they walking straight into the lion's den? Taking an unnecessary risk? Keith would never forgive himself if something bad happened on his watch. The reasons extended far beyond professional ones. The more he got to know Amaya, the more protective he felt of her and the more he wanted to help reclaim her life. This was becoming personal for him. Could he risk getting emotionally involved with his first client? Wouldn't that tank his career before it got off the ground?

Would it matter if he lost her?

Whoa there, Firebrand. You better get a handle on your feelings toward Amaya.

Was it that simple?

10

The library was comprised of two buildings, but Amaya followed Keith into the Jesse Jones structure. The façade was angular and modern juxtaposed against the ornate buildings surrounding it. A sign revealed the library closed on Sundays. She searched her memory from a year ago to determine whether or not she and Loralee—if that was really her name—had exchanged e-mails on that day.

A faint memory of Loralee saying she took one day off a week surfaced. Could she have been referring to Sundays? Heck if Amaya could remember. Not only had she slept since then, but what started out as a what-if project had blossomed into a viable business. Almost viable. The rug was pulled out from underneath her even faster but she didn't want to focus on that right now.

It wasn't lost on her that downtown Houston housed the jails, along with criminal and civil courthouses for the county. She'd checked online using Keith's phone to learn there was a federal prison and courthouse.

Was his mother housed near here?

The Jesse Jones building was also called the Central Library, which was probably easier for most people to remember.

Amaya surveyed every face as she walked past, looking for a moment of recognition or for someone to immediately turn an about-face. Wouldn't Loralee look guilty if she almost bumped right into the person she'd sent those horrible message to?

Loralee's phone had been disconnected after sending the ugly texts. The cops shrugged it off as her most likely blocking Amaya from sending any messages or reaching out to her old PA. It was a common practice apparently. Amaya got it, even though it stung to have it happen to her. She'd used the block button on exes when they didn't seem to want to let go, but not on friends or people from work. Then again, Amaya didn't have many people who were close to her, and she didn't socialize with anyone from past jobs except Marky.

She didn't think she'd upset anyone enough for them to want to physically harm her. Would people in her life have described her as cold?

There was no denying that she came into work, did her job, and left with as little social interaction as possible. To an outsider, she might come across as conceited. In actuality, her mind was always spinning on ways to get out of the life she'd been born into. Her brain churned almost nonstop on trying to figure out a way to change her circumstances. She hadn't given much thought as to how that might come across to others until now.

The bold colors of the interior of the library hit her as she walked inside. The fact that it would be easy to slip in and out of a place like this struck her too. The place bustled, even past ten o'clock on a weekday. She often wondered what kind of job people worked when she did a Starbucks run in the middle of the day. There was almost always a line at the one near her apartment. People filled up most of the tables too at all times during the day.

Now that everyone had gone back to offices to work, even if on a flexible basis, she couldn't figure out what people did to have that kind of freedom every day. There were only so many Realtors who were out and about. Vacations could account for some of the traffic.

But this building, much like Starbucks, had a wide variety of people wandering around on the grounds, sipping a latte with a book in hand. Children were out and about too. How many were homeschooled these days?

Couldn't be this many, could it?

The biggest question was where to start in the multistory building.

Amaya studied each face as she passed by person after person. She discounted mothers or fathers with children. Her logic was Loralee hadn't mentioned anything about a child. Ever. Not one casual comment of picking up a kid after school or needing to take a little one to a swim or gymnastics class. No baseball or other sports.

She reminded herself Loralee might be a man. Her mental image of who she believed her PA to be was definitely a stumbling block. It made sense, though. If she was going to trick someone by using a false identity while hiding behind a computer screen, wouldn't it throw people off more to change her sex?

Then, there were people who identified as a different sex. They might be in the body of a male but feel in their hearts they should have been born a female. Someone with that conviction might seek out the sanctity of a computer screen to hide behind if they weren't comfortable coming out as a different sex.

Then there were just plain criminals out there, who were better at taking from others when they were safely hidden, tucked in a room. Did Loralee think Amaya would get comfortable enough to share banking information? If Amaya wrote a check for payroll, her data would be right there for the recipient to steal, easy-peasy. Wasn't there a data entry job/scam that sent a check for the candidate to cash in order to 'buy their own equipment' but in truth the check would bounce and the scammer would have critical account numbers?

Killian had almost been caught in that snare when he first got out of jail. Luckily, he'd asked to use her address since he was staying at a shelter. He'd popped up out of the blue with the request, excited that he could work from home and the company was going to supply the equipment needed.

Her brother wasn't naïve. He'd been desperate to find a job and stand on his own two feet after being locked up and essentially told he was worth nothing. Amaya had asked why he'd waited to contact her but he'd shrugged the question off like it was no big deal.

She'd offered to let him stay with her in her studio apartment but he'd refused. Jail hardened him. He had an edge to his personality that had never been there before. The funny side to him subdued. He'd been barely nineteen when he'd gone in.

Time changed a person.

"Wish I knew what I was looking for," she whispered to Keith, who kept hold of her hand. The link offered a calm reassurance.

"We have a name," he said, glancing over at the counter

where a pair of workers were at opposite ends typing on computers.

"What about Simon?" she asked.

"I'm sure he's working on that angle as we speak," he said. "Since I've never been a patient man, nor have I relied on one person, I'd like to try to squeeze behind the counter and see what we can find."

"What are the chances they'll both go on break at the same time?" she asked.

"My fear exactly," he agreed. "It's not likely. Of course, if one of them left the counter the other one could be distracted by one of us."

"Since they're both women, you'll probably have better luck than I will," she said. Most of the women they'd walked past so far gave him more than a passing glance. She'd noticed even though he seemed oblivious.

"I don't know about that," he said with more of that characteristic down-to-earth charm.

Did he seriously not know how hot he was?

Amaya suppressed a smile.

He had to be blind not to see the women watching his every move. They might be keeping him in their peripheral but they were looking.

"Let's break up and browse," Keith suggested. "If you see one of them leave, get into position and I'll do my best to distract the other one."

Amaya squeezed his hand for fortitude. "Be careful."

∽

Keith was not only watching the front counter folks, but he was keeping an eye out to see if anyone appeared surprised by Amaya's presence in the library or particularly interested in her in general. Based on what happened at the hotel, he couldn't rely just on recognition as a warning sign. Folks recognized her, so anyone performing a double take might just be curious if she was who they thought. He'd been at a rodeo once that was attended by Bradley Cooper. Folks could've given themselves whiplash for how fast they turned their heads over and over again to verify what they believed was true. Bradley Cooper was in the house.

Rumor had it the man had been researching a role and trying to walk around incognito in a cowboy hat, jeans, and boots.

If not for the rubber-neckers, Keith could have walked right past the man without noticing him. But he'd never been overly starstruck by anyone. He rarely got out to the movies, preferring to wait until he could be comfortable in his own home.

It had been a long time since he'd had someone over for movie night, even though he liked kicking back with the right person.

Keith tried not to draw attention to himself as he skimmed the perimeter of the room, moving from shelf to shelf. Hell if he knew if this approach would work. Going to the computer section without knowing what Loralee looked like didn't seem like the move.

Again, he could watch everyone in the room for their reaction to seeing her. What would it do? Reveal someone recognized her? Covering someone who had a recognizable face was far more challenging than he'd imagined.

There were roughly two dozen adults in the library, with a handful of children milling around. Tables set at the end of bookshelves, close to a window, housed another dozen or so who were sprinkled around the perimeter. Some with backpacks. Others with laptops. It was like a Starbucks without the coffee bar or Gen Z baristas calling out random names, looking like they could care less if customers were there or not. The disinterest from nose-pierced employees was part of the ambience.

No one seemed particularly interested in Amaya so far. He was both relieved and disappointed, a bizarre mix of emotions.

The clerks stood dutifully behind the counter, studying their screens and typing like kids with smartphones in restaurants while their parents tried to have a conversation. Most folks, he'd noted, seemed annoyed by their children when out. He wondered why they didn't hire a babysitter or hit up the grandparents for a night out.

Then again, from what he'd heard, kids came with a hefty price tag in and of themselves. So parents lugged them around to restaurants that bored the kids and made the parents order a second round of drinks to get through dinner.

Once again, he didn't see the point of having children if that was the case. Why bring someone into this world that you didn't want to carry around with you for the foreseeable future? That was the job of parenting. It wasn't like this was a big secret.

Keith acknowledged his view of parents and parenting was most definitely tainted by his own family situation. He was aware his mother hadn't had the best upbringing. Wouldn't that make the thought of having a family less appealing? She did go on to have nine children. He was still scratching his head over that move.

A tall guy with a decent build stood to one side pretending to be interested in a book, but was watching Amaya out of the corner of his eye. The guy's expression had a predatory quality to it that raised Keith's defenses.

It occurred to Keith the guy looked like he was about to walk over and hit on Amaya. Good luck with that, he thought. She wasn't easy prey and wouldn't take lightly to a jerk coming onto her.

Compliment her and she turned six shades of red. But a direct come-on with a cheesy line would go over about as well as spitting in her salsa.

Like he'd thought, good luck with that maneuver, dude.

Still, Keith kept his eye on the man. He didn't like him one bit. The tall guy had on white linen pants with a black button-down short-sleeved shirt. The hem was white and it had a front pocket. The top three buttons of the shirt were left unbuttoned revealing a tanned, hairy chest. Okay, the dude had a few muscles. Who cared?

He also wore a gold Italian horn necklace.

The whole outfit made it look like he was trying a little too hard to come off as casual. He had on some kind of boat shoes. What was he supposed to be...crew? Dark brown, almost black hair was just long enough to curl at the edges. He had a thick head of hair. Keith would give him that. And just enough hair on his chin to make the mustache not look like a seventy's porn star stache.

The man looked like he was trying to give off the impression he had money. It was another move Keith never understood. When he met someone—correction *if* he met someone—the last thing he would want to do was reel them in with his checkbook.

Unless it was the real deal and a woman fell in love with him for the *real* him, and not just because he had a bunch of zeroes in a bank account, he couldn't be bothered. Because he didn't care if the woman he fell in love with had money. Money didn't curl up in bed and keep him warm at night. He wasn't saying it didn't provide a roof over his head or that it wasn't important. It was also how he put food on the table. He knew enough to be thankful that he didn't have to worry about trying to get it. Although, to be fair, he'd be just as happy sleeping under the stars every night in a tent.

A little voice in the back of his head pointed out that was all fine and dandy until the temperature dropped below 32 degrees and he was freezing his balls off every time he stepped out of the tent to empty his bladder.

Or how much he enjoyed coming back to his small place and lighting a fire after being out in the elements for days on end while hunting poachers.

Alright, he could admit living out on the range would get old, if that was his only choice. A hot shower after a cold day was the closest thing to heaven he figured he'd ever see. Except, of course, if he considered Amaya. She had the looks of an angel and he was certain God himself would agree.

Amaya tilted her head as she skillfully scanned the room. If he wasn't locked onto her right now, he would have missed the eye sweep. She would make a good investigator or undercover agent.

Her gaze skimmed past Mr. Trying Too Hard. He didn't seem to get the memo that she wasn't interested.

The man locked in on Amaya, as if she were prey. And then, like a fool, decided to make his move.

11

Oh no, that cheesy smile, linen-wearing man wasn't making his way toward Amaya, was he? Except he was. Great. From the corner of her eye, she noticed Keith watching the situation. She took great comfort in having someone watch her back for a change. Linen Pants didn't seem to notice anyone else in the room, including Keith. Then again, another man might size him up but wouldn't gawk at him like half the women were doing.

Okay, gawk might be a strong word.

Amaya would chalk her sensitivity up to feeling vulnerable if she could. Her sharp mind let nothing get past it. She was defensive because she liked the man. More than liked. But this wasn't the time to get inside her head about it as Linen Pants walked up full of swagger.

"Hey," he said, motioning toward the book in her hand. Unfortunately, she didn't realize she'd been holding it upside down. "It's probably better that way, huh?" He laughed at his own joke.

"Not today, buddy," she said, figuring standing here with

Linen Pants only drew attention toward her. From the corner of her eye, she saw one of the clerks pick up a book, study the spine, and then leave her post.

This was the perfect time...or would have been if Linen Pants wasn't crowding her. The man was full of himself.

"Then when?" he asked, touching his finger to her hand. Not only was there a complete lack of electricity, she felt ice instead. There was nothing sexy about that. Or him.

Thankfully, Keith sauntered over to her and kissed her on the cheek. He righted the book in her hand and then turned to Linen Pants. "Thanks for keeping my girlfriend company while I found what I was looking for." He held up the book in his hand. "I've got this from here on out though."

Linen Pants took a step back as he sized Keith up and seemed to decide not to provoke. He put his hands up in mock surrender. "You probably shouldn't leave a beautiful woman like that standing alone for too long. I wouldn't if she was my girl."

There was so much wrong with that statement that Amaya didn't even know where to start. It was a sexist thing to say and she wasn't anyone's 'girl,' by the way. She could hold her own physically, mentally, and emotionally with everyone, male or female.

Her free hand fisted. She had to force her fingers to relax.

Keith smirked before looping an arm around her waist. He didn't speak. Instead, he looked ready to enjoy the show of whatever came out of her mouth next.

Time was of the essence so she didn't fully engage. "Move on before I give you a piece of my mind."

She was pretty certain he mentioned something about getting a piece of another one of her body parts, but she had to let that comment go too as much as it pained her. This jerk wasn't worth a response.

Instead, she wrapped her arms around Keith's neck and pressed her lips against his. She arched her back enough that her body was flush with his. He was a solid wall of a man. Sexy. And he tasted like a mix of dark roast and peppermint toothpaste. Her new favorite mix.

The kiss heated up in a matter of seconds, catching her off guard. His hand splayed against the small of her back, pressing her against him until she could feel his heart racing. It matched the tempo of hers.

Electricity crackled in the air around them as her breath quickened. A moment of clarity struck that the kiss might be drawing unwanted attention even though it had been the perfect revenge for Linen Pants to see.

Keith pulled back a second before she meant to. He rested his forehead against hers and took a moment to catch his breath. She appreciated the move because she too needed a moment. If just kissing this man was this amazing, she could only imagine what having sex would be like. Instinct said it would be a game-changer.

Was she ready for that? Would she ever be ready for someone to rock her world emotionally and physically? Because she was beginning to realize that Keith Firebrand was capable of doing that and so much more...

Their opportunity passed as the second clerk returned to her post. Amaya locked gazes with Keith. He looked resigned to the same thing she was thinking. They were making no progress.

With a quick nod, they turned in opposite directions and meandered through the room. She ran her finger along the books, wondering how many words and ideas were housed inside these walls. It was cool when she really thought about it.

Walking down aisle after aisle until her legs were tired and her stomach growled, she finally met back up with Keith. "It's not happening. Maybe we should duck out for a little while so we can refuel."

"Food sounds good about now," he agreed.

The trip might have been fruitless, but it was better than sitting around in a hotel room like a sitting duck. It would have only been a matter of time before more folks gathered once word spread. And then what?

The killer would have been in the crowd?

It already creeped her out to no end the person could have possibly been there and she didn't realize it. And then there was her father. Would he wish harm on her? The man had definitely failed as a parent to both of his children.

They walked out into the blazing sun and kept going a couple of blocks to the nearest café. Houston Eats Café was a bustling eatery with a bright atmosphere. Keith requested a booth in the back corner and was granted his wish.

The booths were made of wood and had high walls in between offering the most privacy. The back corner booth was practically its own island, for how far away it seemed from the hustle and bustle of the main dining room, a room that was filled with four-top tables.

Amaya slid into the booth with her back to the room. Keith took the bench seat opposite her. This way, no one would recognize her. Considering Keith was a Firebrand, and she now realized what that meant, she couldn't guarantee people wouldn't know him.

A waiter came and took their drink orders after placing two waters down. She picked her glass up and polished off the contents in a matter of seconds. "I didn't realize how thirsty I was."

"Do you want mine?" Keith asked, picking up the glass and holding it toward her.

"No," she said. "You drink it. They'll bring more."

He nodded and set the glass down on the wooden table.

"I've been thinking about my father showing up at the hotel," she said. "What are the odds he wasn't following us already?"

"It's possible," Keith said but his expression said he doubted it.

"You think we would have noticed?" she asked.

"We drove at night on major roads and highways," he rationalized. "Anything's possible."

"Which means he would have had to have been following Killian and I," she reasoned. She bit her lip and then shook her head. "It doesn't make sense, does it?"

"Does your father have a connection to the hotel where we stayed?" Keith asked.

"Not unless he worked as a busboy," she quipped. "He doesn't exactly have a track record of employment. Then again, I haven't spoken to the man in years."

"It's possible he caught wind of someone trying to hurt you and wanted to see for himself that you were okay," he offered.

"In a perfect world, my father would want the best for me," she said. "That's just not my experience with him and that's all I have to go on."

"People rarely change," he agreed.

"While we're here, do you want to check on your mother?" Amaya asked. Her question caught him off guard.

A hurt look darkened his features. The look broke her heart into pieces.

Keith wasn't sure why he reacted to Amaya's question the way he did. "I thought I was better about the situation with my mother. The thought of going to see her now that I'm in Houston is throwing me off."

Amaya reached across the table and touched his hand with the kind of tenderness that made him want to switch benches and sit beside her.

"I'm sorry, Keith. That was a curveball you weren't expecting. We were talking about parents and I randomly thought about your mother. I thought about her while we were on the way over here from Austin. And, if I'm honest, I thought about her while we were in the library too."

"Why?" he asked, curious.

"I don't know," she responded before tucking her hair behind her right ear. "I've just been thinking a lot about family since seeing my father. You've been helping me out so much, and I guess part of me would like to do the same for you."

He looked up to catch her studying his reaction.

"My plan was to swing by the jail and see her," he said honestly. "But the thought of actually seeing her, helpless, in one of those orange jumpsuits..."

Keith didn't normally get emotional. He wasn't the kind of person who wore his emotions on his sleeve or needed to sit for hours and talk about his feelings. Besides, these had been tucked down so deep he believed it would be impossible to locate them again.

Boy, was he wrong.

They'd been lying in waiting like a panther. Crouching low in a dark place, waiting for the right time to lunge. And now he had no idea how he could face his mother when there wasn't a damn thing he could do to get her out of there.

"It's awful to imagine," she reassured. "In fact, my imagination would be running wild just thinking about it. You don't have to go or do anything you don't want to, Keith. Whatever you decide is fine. You don't owe anyone else anything."

He did, but that was beside the point.

"It feels wrong to turn my back on family when someone is down," he finally said before the waiter interrupted.

"What can I get for you?" the youngish guy who looked too old to still be in college but way under thirty asked Amaya.

"Cheeseburger and fries," she said. "And a strawberry milkshake."

"I'll have the same," Keith said. "But I'll take a coffee with mine."

"Then bring two straws," she interjected.

The waiter tapped their order into a small handheld device, thanked them, and then promised more water for Amaya. Staying hydrated was smart so he drank half his water glass once hers was refilled.

"You have a lot of honor, Keith. It's part of the reason I respect you so much. You're an honest person and it's easy to see family is important to you. But there's no rulebook for the kind of stuff you're dealing with. You should go lighter on yourself."

Could he? Could he give himself a break? Could he walk away from Houston without visiting his mother?

"You don't have to be perfect," Amaya pointed out. "No one is. And families can be messy. Believe me."

He nodded agreement there.

They weren't so different the two of them. Not where it counted.

"I appreciate what you're saying," he started. "And I've decided to swing by the jail. It's time to put on my big boy pants and face what I can't fix. As frustrating as that might be. It'll be worse if I leave the city without following through on my plan to visit.

"I'll be right there beside you if you want or waiting in the truck," Amaya said. "You don't have to do this alone."

Damned if those words didn't strike him in the middle of the chest full force. Despite being almost constantly surrounded by family, he'd always felt alone.

"I'll take you up on that offer," he said to her, wondering if he could open the door just a little to let her in. That kiss back in the library had been life-altering. He'd never experienced so much intensity and passion in one kiss before. So much promise. His body ached for more. His fingers ached to reach out to her and touch her. And his mouth ached to cover those lips of hers.

"Okay then," she said with a self-satisfied smile that managed to be both sexy and sweet at the same time. "It's settled."

The food came. They ate in quiet companionship. Shared the strawberry milkshake that was better than any milkshake had a right to be.

Amaya yawned twice once plates were cleared and her belly was full. She reached over and picked up his coffee cup before taking a couple of sips. It wasn't still warm at this point but she didn't seem to mind.

"Is it bad we came all this way and I'm not ready to go back into the library?" she asked after the third yawn.

"You're tired," he said.

"The timing is terrible," she said on a shrug. "I'll be alright. I can handle missing a night of sleep."

"Except that you've missed more than that," he pointed out.

She smiled at him with a look that said it couldn't be helped. The adrenaline that had kept her going had long since faded. She was eating. It was only a matter of time before tiredness would catch up to her.

"I can get a hotel room," he offered.

"What good would it do? They might find us again and end up running us out." She took another sip of coffee. "I'll get my second wind."

He had another idea. "You can always sleep in the truck while I drive around."

"No," she countered. "I'll be fine."

Looked like Keith was about to come face to face with his mother. Given his upbringing, he'd never been concerned with whether or not he could handle a situation...until now.

12

Twelve Hundred Baker Street housed upwards of four thousand inmates. In the six-story, maximum security rated building, surprise visits weren't allowed. Visitors were supposed to pre-register on the jail's website and visits were granted based on a schedule that considered things like the floor and day.

Keith hid his disappointment at being turned away. Jackie Firebrand's floor got Wednesdays, so he registered for the next day at nine o'clock in the morning, which was the same time the library opened. Since they needed a place to stay for the night, Keith called in a favor from a family friend and asked for discretion.

The three-story light blue with white trim home on Campeche Court was a stone's toss from Pirate's Beach in Galveston. It took just under an hour and a half to make the drive. Two levels' worth of balconies positioned to take advantage of the view were furnished with rocking chairs on one and a long table with chairs on the other. A gas grill sat on the balcony that had the table, ready to grill at a moment's notice.

Amaya pictured big family dinners on the deck, after a long and exhausting day of fun on the beach. She saw laughter as the bright orange orb descended into a peaceful sleep but not before painting the clouds as it waved goodnight.

The interior of the open concept living, dining, and kitchen area walls were painted white wainscotting. The interior colors were sea blues and greens, calming and yet somehow vibrant. Seashells in various shapes and sizes were sprinkled around the rooms.

They arrived by three o'clock, stomachs full and road tired. Or maybe just tired. Amaya hadn't had sleep other than a nap here and there since this whole ordeal started three days ago. Her life had blown up so sleep was the last thing on her mind. The lack of it was catching up to her.

This home had four bedrooms, two of which had double bunk beds. The master had a king-sized bed and the secondary bedroom had a queen. Amaya set her overnight bag down there and walked into the kitchen, where Keith sat at the bar-height counter. He sat on a stool, elbows resting on the counter, hands clasped together.

"Move your stuff to the master," he said, opening his eyes. He must have been deep in thought. She regretted disturbing him.

Amaya shook her head. "The bedroom down the hall is fine. Plus, we're only planning to be here for one night, right?"

"This could be a good base if we need to be close to Houston," he said, turning to face her. He nodded toward the stool beside his.

She slid onto the seat, kicked her shoes off, and pulled her feet up.

Looking around, she couldn't help but wonder who had

friends like this. Keith Firebrand. That was who. To be able to make a call and then gain access to a place like this based on a favor was beyond her wildest imagination. It blew her mind.

As it turned out, he was from one of the most influential families in Texas and she'd had no idea who he was. She'd been rude to him when they first met, thinking he was way too young for the job of keeping her alive.

Amaya would laugh at herself now. She'd been jacked up on adrenaline and fear, rejecting every idea Killian had come up with until he literally forced her into her Range Rover and made the drive to Lone Star Pass. She'd resisted leaving her apartment, thinking it might be safer to hole up there. Digging her heels in on that one had lasted all of five seconds when she'd realized how ridiculous she was being. Having an attempt on her life didn't make her the best critical thinker.

Where was Killian now? What was her brother doing?

Speaking of people, she needed to get hold of Marky. He was bound to be worried sick at this point, considering she'd disappeared without a word and her cell phone was gone. News would travel to him fast about what happened to her and her business.

"I was just thinking that I'd like to reach out to Marky and see what he knows about what happened," she said to Keith.

"It's a good idea," he agreed.

"Except for the fact we can't use your cell phone to make the call," she said.

"No, we can't."

"Do you have another suggestion then, because I'm all out of ideas," she admitted.

"I thought about swinging by the store to pick up a burner phone," he said.

She cocked an eyebrow unsure what that was.

"It's a non-traceable line," he clarified.

"If Marky doesn't recognize the number, he'll let the call go straight to voicemail."

"Will he listen to it though?" he asked. "On second thought, you could always text first to let him know it's you."

"The other problem is that I have no idea what his cell number is," she realized. "I'm sure I knew that before at some point. Maybe." She bit back a yawn. "My brain is starting to shut down."

"Get some rest," he urged. "My friend has food stocked in the fridge and the cabinets, so we don't have to leave."

An idea dawned on her. "I know where Marky works. He'll be on shift later this evening. Once the dinner rush slows down, I can call the restaurant and ask the hostess to put him on the phone."

"That'll work," Keith confirmed with a small smile. She liked being the one to put it there even if it didn't reach his tired eyes.

"Hey, I can stay here with you and talk," Amaya offered.

"Don't worry about me," he said. "Besides, I'll be here when you wake up."

Amaya thought about her next words carefully. "I have a favor to ask, if you don't mind."

"Anything," he said, searching her eyes. "Name it."

Did she have a right to ask more of him?

The short answer was no.

And yet, he probably needed to rest almost as much as her. Steeling her resolve, she took in a deep breath. "You have every right to say no, so I don't want you to feel any sort of pressure about what I'm about to ask. Okay?"

She searched his eyes—eyes that she could so easily get lost in but wouldn't. She couldn't allow herself to fall into the trap of opening her heart to Keith, or anyone for that matter.

He studied her. Concern wrinkled his forehead. "Deal. Ask away."

"I won't be offended if you say no," she reassured. "Because this is a big ask."

Keith searched her eyes for a clue as to what she was about to ask. Why was it so difficult to come out with her request?

Because she cared about his response, his possible rejection, in a way that she'd never cared about someone's before. Because he could crush her so easily with his words in a way no one had ever done before. Because she was vulnerable when it came to Keith Firebrand in a way she'd never experienced before.

Since she'd delayed as long as she could, she decided to come right out with the request. "Will you come lie down with me?"

Amaya tensed, readying herself for the blow.

∽

"Yes, but we're moving into the master bedroom." Keith figured this was the worst of ideas, but the pleading look in those magnetic eyes that saw into his soul wasn't something he could turn down.

"Not a problem," she said, and was up and off the stool before reason could step in and he could change his mind.

Amaya disappeared down the hallway, her gait visibly lighter.

Keith, on the other hand, felt like they were walking in

circles. Nothing had been accomplished today. He picked up his phone and checked the screen. There were messages on the family group chat. But, hey, they were stacking up anyway. He stopped reading those weeks ago when details of the prison beating had been shared. Not being able to do anything to protect his mother, along with the deep-seated feeling he was failing the family by not being able to engage or jump to her defense in arguments, kept him twisted up.

How the hell was he supposed to face the other side of the family after what his mother had done?

Not that any of his cousins had pointed the finger at Keith or his siblings. But Kellan, the oldest, was stepping up to represent Keith and his siblings, and he couldn't help but think it was a mistake considering the bad blood. Their cousin Corbin had been friends with Liv Holden since the third grade. Best friends. In fact, the two had been practically joined at the hip. When Liv's mother died and Corbin had his head up his rear end, some say Kellan swooped in and married Liv, taking advantage of her when she was hanging on by a thread. Needless to say, this didn't go over with Corbin well.

The whole situation became messy. Then, Corbin came back into the picture and, of course, he and Liv ended up reuniting. She'd already left Kellan and was in the process of divorce but Keith's older brother didn't see it quite that way. Kellan must have believed the two of them would get back together and work out their marriage.

Instead, Liv and Corbin are now married and, by all accounts, happy as larks. Kellan said he understood and gave them his blessing at some point, but Keith knew his older brother well enough to know he held a grudge.

Both sides of the family were trying to get along, but

there'd been enough incidents like with Liv and Corbin to keep some level of tension.

It was the reason Keith wanted to strike out on his own despite how much he loved the ranch and the land where he grew up. Making a success of himself ranked right up there with never going back on his word once given.

Keith shook his head wondering when life got so complicated. Being the youngest out of all the family members, he'd been sheltered from plenty of the drama occurring amongst the older set in the family. Kellan and their cousin Adam seemed to butt heads from the time they were born six months apart. This side of the family had the oldest by six months and the youngest by two years, Keith.

Keith had never been close to his parents and he preferred it that way, based on the few interactions they'd had. The Marshall had been a stoic old man who'd done nothing but wreak havoc on relationships he'd strained in the first place.

The picturesque big family with holiday meals in the big house were nonexistent. But then Keith didn't know any different either. If he had kids, which was a big if, he would use an entirely different blueprint to raise them. He was already seeing his brothers and cousins start families and do better.

Then again, the bar was low when it came to parenting and Firebrands.

Pushing up to standing, he checked his cell phone screen one more time hoping for a small miracle from Simon. Luck wasn't on his side today. The library had been a bust. The jail hadn't worked out as he'd hoped. The only good things right now were Amaya and this beach house.

They had a plan for her to reach out to her friend Marcus, who she referred to as Marky. Keith couldn't get behind calling a grown adult Marky. He couldn't help but wonder if it was some kind of pet name. Had the two of them dated?

The thought put Keith in a sour mood. Talking to Amaya's ex wasn't high on his list of things he looked forward to. She'd been coy about the nature of their relationship, saying they didn't always get along, which generally meant exes who tried to stay friends after a breakup. The logic was that they'd loved each other once and that love didn't just disappear. However, seeing an ex with a new boyfriend or girlfriend was never easy and he didn't see how two people wanted to sign up for that particular brand of torture.

Maybe they didn't really love each other to begin with. Casual dating could lead to casual friendships. But he wasn't the casual type. Could he be intense about his feelings? The short answer there was hell yes. Was it the reason he didn't do serious relationships? Also, hell yes.

Keith wasn't likely to change anytime soon either, which was the reason he needed to keep Amaya at arm's length. She was easy to talk to. The term easy on the eyes came to mind too, but that didn't nearly do her justice.

She had a lot of little quirks, he'd noticed, that made her even more alluring. Like the way she played with her hair when she let her guard down; the way she scraped her teeth across her bottom lip, leaving a silky trail when she was thinking hard on something; the way she tilted her head to one side when she was really listening, and those adorable little wrinkles in her forehead when she concentrated.

Amaya was exactly the kind of woman Keith could see himself with for the long haul. He could see a few kids running around the ranch, like he'd done for much of his childhood. He could see the two of them falling hopelessly in love. The picture-perfect kind, except real.

He knew one thing, if he had someone like Amaya, he'd cherish her for the rest of his life.

Keith cleared his throat and refocused on the screen. It was probably a good thing he didn't do the whole falling-in-love bit. It wouldn't work out like the vision in his head anyway. Did these things ever work long-term?

A little voice in the back of his mind picked that moment to point out many of his brothers and all of his cousins had found love, real love. The kind that had them completely enthralled with their partners. Several of them had started families or become one. Others found out they already had kids they never knew about for one reason or another, and stepped up to be the father they'd never had.

Alright, fine. Love worked out for some. It even managed to work out for Firebrands. Still, Keith wasn't convinced it would ever be the right play for him no matter how drawn he was to Amaya.

He shook his head trying to empty his thoughts. And then he sent a name to Simon. Puddin' Pop.

The response came back almost immediately. *On it.*

Looking toward the master, Keith tucked his phone away and headed toward the bedroom where Amaya had moved her overnight bag.

13

Amaya had already freshened up in the bathroom by the time Keith came into the bedroom. The house was beautifully decorated and this room was no exception. The bed looked like a white puffy cloud against a pale blue sky; it reminded her of sitting outside and looking at the sky. She might not be an outdoors girl at heart, but that didn't mean she couldn't enjoy a beautiful sunset or a gorgeous spring day.

Besides, the sky at night was a wonder, with its dark blue velvet canopy dotted with brilliant fire bursts in the form of stars. Who wouldn't get lost gazing up at something as mesmerizing as that?

The light on the nightstand was turned to its lowest setting, casting the room in a dark glow. Amaya had changed into pajamas, brushed her teeth, and was now slipping underneath the covers of the soft as a cloud bed.

Keith made a beeline for the bathroom without saying a word. Was he just tired or dreading getting into bed with her? No need to get on that hamster wheel. She could spin herself out trying to figure out someone else's motivation. Besides, as tired as she was, her brain was overclocked.

Amaya yawned for the third time since climbing into bed. Her sleep schedule had been nonexistent in the past couple of years as she'd worked day and night to build her business. There'd been no separation from work and home, which made sense given the fact she had no money for a studio. It also made waking up in the middle of the night with an idea easy to hop out of bed and try.

She'd done that more times than she could count.

What about tomorrow? What about when rent came due? Trying to live on intermittent payments when her small nest egg had dwindled hadn't been easy. She'd discovered more ways to cook ramen to make it into a meal than she could count. Throw an egg in, along with some bell peppers, mushrooms, and tofu, and she had a meal. Siracha gave it all the heat she needed. Other times she tossed in Bok choy when she could find and afford it.

The downtown Dallas farmers' market was a great place to find fresh vegetables that didn't cost an arm and a leg. Considering she was only one person, it wasn't too hard to pull together a meal. Marky brought over leftovers when he could from the restaurant. She'd learned to shop places that sold day-old bread for the best deals. Freeze a loaf in time and she was good to go for weeks with a jar of peanut butter. Throw in jelly and she was over the moon.

Life had been getting easier lately, though. The small sponsorships started paying the rent and allowing her to buy better groceries. What was the saying? One step forward and two steps back.

Why did life have to work that way?

Keith slipped in behind her and turned off the light. The

mattress dipped underneath his weight. His warmth and spicy scent filled the room.

"Thank you for staying with me," Amaya said softly. In this moment, she felt more vulnerable than she could ever remember. "I hope it isn't too much of an inconvenience."

"None," he said, his voice low and husky.

Was she having the same effect on him? A growing piece of her hoped so even though nothing serious could come of it. What would a flirtation hurt?

That annoying voice in the back of her mind reminded her a man like Keith could cause permanent damage to her heart.

"Hey," he said with the deep timbre that traveled all over her and through her. "I'm lying here because I want to be next to you. And I'd really like to hold you in my arms."

"What's stopping you?" she asked, rolling over to face him and snuggle into the crook of his arm. She felt peaceful for the first time since this whole ordeal started. It wouldn't last. Couldn't. Someone out there wanted to kill her. Taking her down wasn't enough. The bastard had tried to poison her, not face her. The move was chicken.

"Nothing, now that you've given me permission," he said as his voice washed over her. She remembered how he'd tasted earlier, all dark roast and peppermint toothpaste.

Keith held her close. He'd taken off his shirt and had on boxers. She liked the feel of his skin against hers, of his body against hers. She liked his warmth and the way his touch was so tender as he made small circles on her shoulder with his fingers and thumb.

She could stay in this spot forever, food be damned. Keith was everything she needed to survive.

Was she being ridiculous? Yes. Starvation would strike

sooner or later and they'd have to get up at the very least to forage for food. Did she want to? No.

"Close your eyes," Keith said quietly.

When she did, he feathered kisses on one eyelid and then the next. He brushed a kiss against her lips, stopping before she could react or tease his tongue inside her mouth, like she very much wanted to do right now.

"You're safe," he finally whispered. "You can rest."

Exhaustion washed over her, making her tired down to her bones. Despite the yawning and the bone-deep weariness, Amaya doubted she could fall all the way asleep. But she closed her eyes anyway.

When Amaya opened her eyes again, it was dark outside. She could see a sliver of moon through the slats in the miniblinds, which was the only light streaming into the space.

Instinctively, she reached around for Keith and found nothing but empty sheets. The bed was cold without him. She sat up and stretched her arms out wide, wondering how long she'd been out. Minutes? Hours?

The clock on the nightstand said it was half past eleven. Had she really just slept a solid eight hours?

Shaking off the fog in her brain, she threw off the covers and forced her legs over the side of the bed. She sat there for a long moment, listening for any signs Keith was in the next room. It was quiet, so she stood up and properly stretched out her arms. She'd been called a spider monkey when she was younger because she'd been all arms and legs with a skinny body.

Thankfully, she'd filled out as she'd gotten older, but gaining weight at her height had never been easy. The fact she'd had very little to eat growing up at times probably didn't help. She'd been teased for being too tall and too skinny. But people loved her for those qualities now. People could be weird.

She'd been asked if she was interested in modeling at one point when she was younger. Funny enough, she didn't trust not having a steady paycheck. Wasn't that a laugh?

At this point, she would chuck all of it for a steady nine-to-five job, as long as her boss didn't chase her around his desk like in the Dolly Parton movie she'd watched on Hulu once. She couldn't imagine that nonsense being allowed in offices now, especially after the #metoo movement.

But then a small family-owned company could probably get away with murder if they wanted to. Jobs weren't all that easy to find, especially good ones with decent pay and benefits. Getting that first job seemed to be hard, even for people who'd taken the traditional college route. That had never been an option for Amaya. She didn't have money to pay for classes and knew how impossible it could be to dig her way out of debt if she took on loans.

Plus, what would she do? Accounting? Were there still jobs working with numbers? Or would she be doing taxes for people or companies for the rest of her life? Since she dreaded doing her own, and put it off until the last minute every year, she figured an accounting degree was out of the question.

Then what?

Get a degree in fashion? Marketing? Neither sounded like they led to a guaranteed income. What about website design? She was good at being an influencer. She liked being behind the camera and was getting good at it.

Being in the spotlight wasn't what it was cracked up to be. When everything was going well and most everyone was supportive—there were always a few trolls out there waiting with snappy comments to counter a positive message or sling an insult from behind the safety of their own computers—the job was amazing. Now? She wouldn't wish it on her worst enemy.

After freshening up in the ensuite bathroom, she meandered out of the room, down the hallway, and toward the kitchen to see what Keith was up to.

She stopped at the mouth of the hallway when she caught sight of him making a cup of coffee with one of those pod-type machines while shirtless and wearing only boxers and jeans slung low on his hips.

Her heart free fell. She was in trouble.

***

The sound of Amaya clearing her throat drew Keith's attention toward the hallway.

"Good morning," he said before twisting his mouth. "Or should I say good evening?"

She walked into the room wearing pajama pants and a tank top. The outfit highlighted those long legs of hers; legs that had been tangled around his a couple hours ago until he gently removed them so he could come into the kitchen and think.

Thinking was impossible while lying next to Amaya, making skin-to-skin contact.

"When did you leave?" she asked, walking beside him.

He caught her gaze to make sure his next move was welcomed. She offered a small smile. If he didn't know her, he would wonder what she was thinking. Now, he had a good idea she was giving him the green light. So, he turned toward her, looped his arms around her waist, and pressed a kiss to full lips.

"I don't care what time of day it is as long as you keep

doing that," she said, widening her smile. He took that as verbal permission to repeat his actions.

The second kiss turned steamy in a heartbeat. She parted her lips and teased his tongue inside her mouth.

Damn.

She tasted like honey with a twinge of mint. Keith could get used to this. Besides, no news had come in, other than Simon saying he had another job in and had to set Keith's work aside for a few hours.

When Keith pulled back this time, his breathing sounded like he'd just gone for a jog. He cracked a smile before turning to hand over the cup of coffee that had just finished brewing. He had to hand it to the maker of pods. They sure made making a good cup of coffee a snap. Although, he missed the smell of a glass carafe and the ease of producing ten cups for his efforts instead of one.

"Here you go," he said, handing over the fresh brew to Amaya.

"That one is yours," she quickly countered, shaking her head. "You did the work, so you deserve the reward."

"Here. Hold this." He handed the mug to her before picking out another pod from a carousel next to the machine. He grabbed a mug from the cabinet located above said machine. "It's this easy to make another cup." He plucked the pod in its spot, tugged the handle toward him until it closed and a light came on. He pressed the lighted button as he placed the mug under the small spout. "Not sure if I can handle doing all this at one time."

She playfully tapped him on the shoulder.

"Alright, Mr. Smarty Pants," she teased. "I'll take this one since you twisted my arm."

"I can think of better things to do with your arm than twist it," he shot back with a wink.

The machine spit and sputtered to make it sound like it was in one of those fancy coffee shops that charge eight dollars for something that can be made for a tenth of the price at home with none of the extra sugar.

He picked up his mug when it was done and took a sip before becoming serious again. "I don't have any news from Simon. He got interrupted and is working on something else. No word on information or an address for Puddin' Pop as of yet."

Amaya frowned, nodded. "At least we have this place for the time being."

For the time being was right. He'd been counting down the hours until they needed to make the drive into Houston. Dreading seeing his mother locked behind bars but also knowing it was time. He needed to do this in order to face it.

They had eight hours before needing to hit the road. Nine and a half hours before he would sit across a plexiglass or table—he had no idea how they would do it—from his mother who was in jail.

Keith let the thought sink in. It sat like a heavy cloak wrapped around his shoulders, weighing him down.

"Hey, what are you thinking about right now?" Amaya asked. She closed the distance between them and traced his cheekbone with her index finger. Her light touch caused his chest to squeeze.

"Facing my mother," he said. "Explaining why I haven't been to see her since this whole ordeal began."

"Maybe you don't owe her an explanation," Amaya said. "And, maybe, she'll just be happy to see you."

"In a perfect world," he said.

"Maybe it will be if only for a few hours," Amaya stated. Her words eased some of the pressure in the center of his chest.

"Are you ready to make the call to your friend?" he asked.

Her eyes widened in shock. "Did you figure out a way to get a burner phone?"

"You'd be surprised at what you can make happen with the Firebrand last name," he said. Keith hadn't used his own name. He'd used Kellan's instead. He figured his older brother owed him one, and no one would be looking for Kellan or associating him with Amaya on the off chance someone besides the hotel worker had recognized him. "I made a call. Paid with cash. The phone was left on the doorstep at the snap of a finger."

"I'm pretty sure my fingers don't work like that," she said. It was meant to be a joke but there was enough awe in her tone to tell him she meant it.

Keith wasn't trying to impress her with his family money. No, he wanted her to like him for who he was instead of his net worth.

And now that she had a burner phone, her friend might be able to shed some light on what was happening in Dallas.

14

"Hello?" Marky's tentative voice came through the line.

"Hi," Amaya said, unsure where to even start. She'd called the restaurant and spoken to Cody, who'd acted strange before giving her Marky's number and saying he could explain.

"Is this really you?" Marky's tentativeness turned into suspicion. Her friend had always been that way. No one ever got one over on Marky, not if he could help it. Did he sometimes get tricked? Sure. Did people at the restaurant go out of their way to test him at times? Definitely yes.

But he was decent at detecting BS when coming face-to-face with it.

"For your birthday last year, I had your cake made into something obscene," she said with a small smile at the memory after putting the call on speaker so Keith could listen in.

"Where are you?" Marky immediately asked.

"That's not important," Amaya said, wondering the same question about him. She didn't have time to get into it with him right now, so she shelved the thought for later. "The main thing is that I'm alive and doing fine."

"But, like, where did you go?" Marky pressed. "I mean, you just, like, disappeared and I had no idea how to get a hold of you or if you were lying in a ditch somewhere. You know what that does to my anxiety."

"I'm okay, Marky."

"What is Killian doing at your apartment?" Marky asked. "I stopped by and he answered the door. He was looking mighty comfortable there, if you ask me."

"He's staying in case the..." She couldn't bring herself to say in case the person who'd tried to kill her came back.

"And you trust him?" Marky's voice sounded weird. Off. Pissed. She'd caused her friend a lot of stress by not immediately reaching out to him. And now he was mad at her.

"Not more than I trust you," she said, trying to smooth things over.

"You know my roommate situation is unlivable," Marky protested. "If you needed someone to stay at your apartment, you could have called me."

"Everything happened so fast," she explained. "Killian was there and suddenly taking charge when I couldn't think straight."

"That's another thing, why was your brother invited in the first place?" Marky went on. He was being unreasonable, which was just like him when he was upset. He was known for focusing on the wrong things.

"Can we focus here," Amaya said, put off by the fact Marky was obsessing over details that had nothing to do with her being alive. "I was almost killed and you're seriously worried about me allowing my brother to stay at my apartment versus you?"

The line was quiet for several beats.

"You're right," Marky conceded in a defeated voice.

"I know that I scared you by disappearing and not resurfacing until now, but it was for the best," she said. "I had to get to safety."

"Which is where?"

Keith caught her gaze and shook his head.

"With a friend," was all she said by way of response, leaving out any other information. "I'm lying low for a few days until this whole thing blows over."

"At least you're alright," Marky said. "What about Killian? Is he planning to stay in your apartment indefinitely?"

Amaya was starting to get annoyed by this line of questioning. "Why do you care so much, Marky? I mean, what's it to you where my brother stays or not."

"Do I have to say it out loud?" Marky sounded indignant.

"I guess you're going to have to spell it out for me because I have no idea what you're getting at," she said, not bothering to hide her frustration at this point. Was Marky so hard up for a place to stay that he would keep harping on this? He wasn't exactly being subtle that he wanted to stay at her place while she was gone.

The line was quiet again. Marky blew out a breath like he was resigned to spelling it out for her.

"Okay, look, I'll say it but don't get mad at me," Marky hedged. The fact he needed to prep her before continuing didn't exactly lower her blood pressure.

"Fine," she said. "I won't get mad. I will, however, be very pissed if you keep talking around whatever it is you have to say. So just come out with it already before I hang up."

"Don't do that," Marky pleaded. "All I'm going to ask is whether or not you truly trust your brother."

"What's that supposed to mean?" she asked, not willing

to go to the place where her brother was responsible for trying to poison her; not even hypothetically could she entertain the thought.

Marky didn't respond.

Her friend was trying to look out for her. Him not wanting Killian staying at her apartment made a lot more sense in this context. "Alright, I understand what you're saying."

"Don't hate me," he said. "It's just that he looked a little too comfortable squatting at your place while you're out, God knows where. What if he wanted you out of the picture and this was the easy way to do it?"

She didn't point out the fact her brother had been the one to bring her to Keith Firebrand for protection. The less Marky knew, the better at this point. Then again, Keith wasn't exactly a known quantity then. He wasn't someone with a track record for protection or doing his job well. But that was because she couldn't afford to pay for protection despite needing it.

Plus, what would her brother do? What was his plan? Run her out of her business and apartment? He'd been the one to show her the ropes to begin with. What would he have to gain by hurting her?

Marky was reaching for something that wasn't there.

"I appreciate you looking out for me, Marky," she began.

"Think about it, okay," Marky pleaded. "And watch your back with him. That's all I'm asking. Don't get me wrong, I'm not saying he's a bad person. Inherently. Desperate people do desperate things sometimes, and you yourself said that he seemed desperate lately."

It was strange how the brain worked once seeds of doubt were planted.

Was it possible Killian would attempt to get rid of her?

Amaya involuntarily shivered at the thought. Her own flesh and blood had turned on her before. Case in point, their father. She still wondered what he was doing showing up at the hotel like that. She should probably give her brother a call to warn him about their father coming out of the woodwork. Or did Killian already know? Were the two of them working together?

"I hear what you're saying," Amaya conceded, not ready to go all in with the theory about her brother.

"So, you'll be careful?"

"I'll watch my back," she promised. Now that those seeds were planted, her brain was trying to work out the reason Killian would want her gone. What would he have to gain if she was out of the picture? It wasn't like she gave him money or that he'd ever asked. He hadn't. In fact, he'd refused her help while living in the halfway house when he first got out of jail. She'd offered a place to stay but Marky didn't know that part of her history with her brother.

"Do you want me to go to your apartment and get rid of him?" Marky asked. "I can hold down the fort while you're gone."

"No," she said, reacting quickly. "I'd rather you leave him alone until this is all figured out."

"Alright then," Marky said.

Since this conversation wasn't going anything like she'd planned, she figured it best to end the call.

"I just wanted to let you know that I'm fine and you shouldn't worry because I'm in good hands," she said to her friend.

"Well, I'm relieved to hear you're not lying in a ditch," Marky said, pouring on the emotion a little thick. Her friend had always been dramatic. His reaction probably shouldn't surprise her. Still, he'd gone down a very different path than expected with this conversation.

"I'm not," she reassured. "So, you can stop worrying about that one."

"I still don't know why you're being so secretive, but okay," Marky said, drawing out the last word. His feelings were definitely hurt. And when Marky's feelings were hurt, everyone knew. He fell into the category of wearing his heart on his sleeve.

She ended the call as Keith caught her gaze.

"I have thoughts," was all he said.

∽

"Marky was definitely off and he was mad that he wasn't included," Amaya started before Keith could say what was on his mind.

Keith didn't immediately speak. Her conversation with her friend raised a few flags but she was in defensive mode right now. And he figured she needed a few minutes to process what just went down. The conversation hadn't gone as planned. He read it on her face during the exchange.

"It was weird," she said, mainly talking to herself but also probably needing to hear herself think by saying the words out loud. "I'm still trying to figure out what's with him." She looked over at him before palming her coffee mug and rolling it around in her hands. Her forehead creased in the way it did when she was concentrating and a little bit frustrated that she couldn't come up with an answer. Or if she was confused.

Keith nodded.

Amaya looked him dead in the eyes. "You said you have

thoughts." She took a sip of coffee that was cold by now and issued a sharp sigh. "Go ahead."

"More like red flags than thoughts," he said.

"Okay, hit me with your concerns."

When she put it like that it sounded like they weren't on the same team. She was defensive about Marky and protective. Keith needed to choose his words carefully.

"My first question is why was he so locked onto you telling him where you were," he said. The man also didn't seem to be terribly shocked she was calling from a burner phone. In fact, he didn't mention it one time, which struck Keith as odd.

"I caught that too," she admitted, biting down on her bottom lip.

"From an outsider's perspective, he seemed more concerned about himself being put out by the fact you'd disappeared, than worried about your well-being."

She started to argue so Keith put his hand up in the surrender position.

"I'm strictly speaking from my point of view," he defended.

Her shoulders were strung tight. Her face muscles tense. She might not want to hear what he was saying, but the call had left her unsettled. His comments seemed to be resonating based on the way she bit down on her lip and tilted her head to one side. She was taking him seriously.

"Go on," she urged.

"He spent a lot of time on the call talking about Killian," Keith pointed out.

"You heard him," she said on an exhale like she'd been waiting for him to bring Killian up. "What do you think about my brother?"

"He was the one who brought you to me for protection,

which doesn't necessarily rule him out," Keith reasoned. "Killian had access to you on the night in question. Correct?"

"So did Marky if we want to get snippy about it," she stated.

Keith reached out to touch her hand. "No one wants to believe someone they love would be capable of harming another human being, let alone themselves. We don't have to talk about him if you don't want to."

"That's the problem, though," she said on another exhale. At least she was breathing. "My mother didn't care enough about me as an infant to stick around. How do you walk away from a tiny, helpless thing? And then my father... well you already know how I feel about him. The timing of him turning up is suspect too, but I haven't even allowed myself to go there. The two most important people in my young life abandoned me and neglected me. Which basically means trusting anyone is..." She blew out a sharp breath. "Let's just say that doesn't come easy for me. So, given my history, is it easy to believe someone close to me would turn on me? Absolutely, yes. Do I want this to be the case? Does it break my heart to think my own brother could turn on me to this degree? Could wish me dead? Could try to kill me?"

Amaya didn't need him to spell out the rest of his thoughts as she set the coffee cup down. She needed him to hold her.

Keith closed the distance between them in one stride and hauled her against his chest where she buried her head and cried.

He offered reassurances that probably rang hollow, despite how much he meant each and every word.

She practically threw her arms around his neck,

clasping her hands together like she was holding on for dear life. Like he was the only thing stopping her from going under and drowning. Like he was the only one she trusted to be her life raft.

Keith couldn't be certain how long they stood there while he held her, and he didn't care. He could spend his whole life like this, if it meant easing some of her pain. Because it was pain he understood a little too well.

In approximately nine and a half hours, he'd be facing his own brand of pain. His mother.

Amaya brought her hands down to wipe her eyes. He feathered kisses on the arch of her brows, her temples, her cheeks.

"I'm sorry," she said, turning her face away from him.

"You don't have to apologize for crying," he said.

"From when I was a little kid, I was smacked if I cried," she said. "It's habit to apologize for, I guess."

"You're safe here, Amaya," he reassured. "I'll never hurt you."

He might never hurt her, but he couldn't say the same for her hurting him. When they exposed who was trying to kill Amaya, they would walk out of each other's lives forever.

And his heart would shatter.

15

Just a few more minutes. Amaya couldn't tear herself away from Keith, from his warmth, from his strength. Leaving him was going to rip her shreds.

When she could, she pulled away and took a step back. She went about quietly fixing a fresh cup of coffee since the last one got cold. And Keith pulled out catered meals from the fridge, already in microwaveable bowls with lids.

While he heated the food—chicken breasts with small containers of doctored up black beans that smelled like heaven—she set the table and fixed coffees. She hated Marky for planting doubts in her mind about her own brother's intentions, but she couldn't ignore them either, if only to prove to herself there was no way Killian would try to harm her.

The two of them had been close at one time. Could jail have changed him to the point she didn't recognize him any longer? There was no arguing he came out a different person. But someone capable of murder?

Amaya also realized she was about to sit down to dinner

with Keith, who was still asking himself the same question about his mother. Jackie Firebrand had pleaded guilty to the charges against her, he'd explained on the drive from Austin to Houston. His mother had recently changed her plea, based on the advice of her new hotshot attorney.

Life sure got complicated in a hurry.

Thinking about Keith's mother as her own father reentered the picture had her wondering if he thought there was money to be had if she was dead. At this point, nothing would shock her. Although, she could still be surprised by others.

Amaya's phone call with Marky had left her feeling worse than when she'd called. Was she missing something with Killian?

They were headed to Dallas after this visit. Should she surprise her brother, stopping by unannounced? She didn't hate the idea. His reaction to her might tell her a lot about where she stood with him.

At least they might get an address to go on for Puddin' Pop if Simon came through. They could expose her identity since she hid behind a silly mask that she held up of—what else?—but a pudding pop. She always distorted her videos which gave a young Katy Perry flare to her work but also made it impossible to get a good read on who she was behind the mask. All the videos were shot using the arm-length feature, distorting the view.

Keith plated the food before bringing it over to the table. He set the plates down and then joined her.

"My mind keeps going over and over the possibility someone from my family could be involved," she said to Keith. He didn't speak the words, but it was obvious Killian was a person of concern at this point. "Has my brother reached out to check on me since handing me over?"

"No," Keith stated. "But that doesn't mean anything. He might be concerned about leaving a trail to you."

This was the answer she wanted to hear whether it was true or not. Amaya had to face facts. Her brother could be behind this or at the very least involved. She couldn't see him working with their father. Killian hadn't mentioned anything about seeing or hearing from the man. To be fair, Killian didn't tell Amaya his every move. He could be keeping secrets from her.

Keith's cell phone dinged, indicating a text message coming through. He stood and walked over the counter before checking the screen. "Simon's back on the case. He's been investigating Puddin' Pop and told me to hold tight. He might have information for us soon."

"Information in the form of...what?"

"Didn't say," Keith responded with a shrug. "I'll take whatever progress we can get right now."

"That's the truth," she agreed.

He rejoined her at the table, leaving his phone on the counter. It was nice to have a conversation with someone without them staring at their phone every five seconds. Marky could be like that. She'd be talking to him and his mind would be on whatever he was reading on his phone.

Keith was one of a kind.

After the meal, Amaya helped clean up and put away dishes. Thankfully, there was a dishwasher at the beach house.

"What should we do next?" she asked.

"I'm game for putting on a movie, if you are," Keith said. "My mind keeps spinning out over not finding the right lead yet, and don't get me started on visitation with my mom tomorrow morning." He checked the clock. "Actually, later today at this point."

"Did you get any sleep before?" she asked.

"I dozed on and off for a while," he admitted. Maybe he could grab a few hours of sleep if they settled in.

"Watching a movie would be a good distraction," she said. "It's weird how doing something normal like heating up dinner and having a meal while sitting at a table, then doing dishes and watching a movie can make you feel human again."

Keith nodded before taking her hand and linking their fingers. "You deserve a break from all this overthinking too."

"Answers never come to me when I'm trying too hard to think about them," she said. It had been that way since as long as she could remember. Distract herself and answers flooded her. Think too hard on trying to figure something out and nada.

Keith linked their fingers before leading her into the living area. A TV covered one wall. Two white sofas faced each other. And a couple of cream-colored chairs with white pillows anchored the room opposite the TV wall. The coffee table was a solid round wood structure. It looked like someone had sanded and smoothed the wood of a massive tree.

He picked up the remote and then sat at the end of one of the couches before positioning Amaya to lean back and rest on his chest. She threw the back pillows off the couch and settled in beside him, back to the crook of his arm where she felt the most safe. He pulled up their options and they decided on a movie about a brilliant math professor who thought he was working for the government, but actually suffered from mental illness.

Three-quarters of the way into the movie, Amaya felt Keith's breathing steady, even out. She clicked off the TV and pulled the blanket off the back of the sofa before finding the crook again. For several hours, she drifted in and out of sleep, letting her mind wander wherever it wanted to go.

And then she fell asleep too.

∽

Keith's eyes opened as the sun bathed the living room in light. He was surprised he'd fallen asleep but probably shouldn't be since he hadn't slept in days. The warm meal, the silky body...the combination had him out like a light before the movie ended.

As soon as he stirred, Amaya opened her eyes.

"Hey," she said. Her sleepy voice tugged at his heartstrings.

He kissed her before she repositioned to sit up next to him. "Good morning."

"What time is it?"

After glancing at the clock behind her on the sofa table, he said, "Almost seven."

"We have to leave in half an hour," she said, rubbing her eyes as she yawned.

Keith pushed up to standing and stretched out his arms. "Seven-thirty it is."

Amaya got up and headed toward the master. "I'll get dressed and be out in half that time."

She had the kind of natural beauty that didn't need a whole lot of fuss.

He joined her in the bathroom to brush his teeth. He'd showered last night so he was good to go there. What should he wear to visit his mother in jail?

Keith threw on fresh jeans and socks. He checked the closet and found a button-down collared shirt that looked to be his size. His friend wouldn't mind if he borrowed it, so he threw it on and buttoned it up.

Amaya came out of the bathroom looking beautiful in a cotton t-shirt dress and heeled boots. He had no idea how she walked in those things but he was certain she could use the heel as a weapon if needed.

"You're beautiful," he said to her.

She smiled and her cheeks turned a few shades of red as she thanked him.

Side-by-side, they worked in the kitchen heating up breakfast burritos and making coffee. He glanced at the clock as he headed toward his phone. "Seven twenty. That has to be some kind of record."

As he picked up his cell, he saw that he had a text message from Simon. "We have an address on Puddin' Pop."

"Oh yeah?" Amaya asked. "Where?"

"It's in Richardson," he said, pulling it up on the map.

"That's a suburb of Dallas. It's just north of the city." Amaya joined him, standing at his side.

"It's a house," he said before catching her gaze. "We might have just found the person whose been harassing you at the very least."

He still wanted to talk to Loralee, but the library idea had turned out to be a bust yesterday. Would they have better luck today or had they hit the clerk's radar and would now be watched too closely? He dismissed the idea. People came and went at the library throughout the day. The little time they'd spent there shouldn't raise any alarms. He was probably just being paranoid. Houston to Dallas was about a four to four and a half hour drive. Galveston to downtown Houston was another hour and a half. They were going to be on the road a lot today.

Also, when he really thought about it, Loralee had

gotten angry with Amaya after the fact. Would she really sabotage Amaya right before she was finally going to get a payout for offering free services for the past year?

But his mind was locked onto something else, his mother. The thought of facing her set him on edge. He had no idea what to expect or if she would even want to see him. He'd taken shifts at the hospital when she'd been in Lone Star Pass to watch over her like his brothers and cousins, but Keith never went inside the room.

Hell, he never made it past the lobby on her floor because he could see her door from where he sat and drank coffee until his time was up.

Did that make him a jerk?

Maybe.

Keith was doing the best he could digesting it all. And now? No more excuses. He was making the drive and going to his visiting session. And then, they'd hit the road again for Dallas. Correction, Richardson.

The thought of taking Amaya back to the place where she'd been targeted reminded him to be cautious. Dot every i. Cross every t. And suspect everyone, including her brother, her friend, and her father.

Amaya searched for news on his phone on the way to the jail. "It looks like Puddin' Pop got the deal I was supposed to sign." Her free hand fisted. She smacked her thigh with it. "That was supposed to be my big break."

"How did she end up signing with them?"

"I'm sure she saw an opportunity and swooped in," Amaya said. "Her followers have gone through the roof, ever since she posted a scathing note about how important honesty is when dealing with the responsibility of having a successful social media channel." Amaya cursed. "I should have been watching her all along. I had a bad feeling something like this would happen."

Business, he knew, could be cutthroat. "I'm sorry that happened, Amaya. Once this is over and you clear your name, you'll be on top again."

"I doubt it," she said. "I heard what you said about people having short memories, but sponsors aren't in the same boat. They remember for a long time, because they can't have their brand tainted by an influencer. Believe me, it's happened. Almost anyone can be a star nowadays."

"How did you get into the business?" he asked.

"Killian showed me," she said. "He was trying to do it himself but couldn't gain a lot of traction. So I learned from him, thinking this would be my side hustle. Then, my followers started climbing. I started posting regularly, twice a day, like clockwork. I hovered around the five thousand mark for a while and then I put out a video that, for reasons I still can't explain, took on a life of its own. It resonated and people shared. Next thing I know I'm sitting at fifty thousand followers." She pinched the bridge of her nose. "That's when people started showing up wanting to work deals. At first, it was exchanging services until I started hitting six-figure followers. My engagement went up too. That's another thing the big sponsors look for. Before I know it, I was being asked to be a brand ambassador, which doesn't always pay in the beginning. Once you start establishing yourself, the money comes in. At first, it's a couple hundred a month. Then, it's a couple thousand. I moved to the penthouse apartment in a building I knew I couldn't afford otherwise. But the building owner said I could rent the first six months for practically a song if I highlighted the building on my story twice a week."

"Sounds impressive," he said. "I heard about someone

who started with an object like a safety pin and traded up until they ended up in a half-million-dollar house."

"Yeah, it works kind of like that," she said. "It just kind of snowballs at some point but no one teaches you how to handle the success or what to do if it all comes tumbling down around you."

Keith couldn't imagine having that kind of instant fame. He'd grown up under the microscope being a Firebrand in Lone Star Pass, but Amaya was dealing with being famous on a whole other level. One that almost got her killed.

Cutthroat might be right.

He pulled into a parking spot downtown a couple of blocks from the jail entrance and cut off the engine. "You don't have to go inside with me if you don't want to. You don't know my mother from Adam, so I'll understand if you want to lay low in the truck. I can do this one on my own if the thought of going inside brings back bad memories from when your brother served time."

"No, Keith. I'm coming in." She reached over and touched his forearm. Contact caused warmth to settle over him, like the warmth of a campfire on a cold night. "I want to meet your family."

She might regret those words.

"Alright then," he said. "Let's do this."

16

Amaya followed Keith through the process of visitation. Jackie Firebrand was being held in a special holding cell, no doubt to keep her safe from other inmates, more than as a punishment.

The visitation would occur in a three-sided metal stall from behind a glass using old-fashioned-looking landlines. Amaya had seen them in pictures, but this was a first in real life. Two plastic chairs had been scooted together, and they were warned if more visitors showed, their time would be cut short. Amaya didn't see how that was fair, given she and Keith had registered in advance, but the stern jailor wasn't someone to be argued with and he didn't look open to negotiations.

They took their seats, Keith closer to the window and Amaya pushed back, and waited for Jackie to be brought to them. Keith's right knee bounced nervously. Amaya reached forward and put her hand on his leg.

He calmed down as he dropped his hand and then linked their fingers.

Jackie Firebrand wasn't at all what Amaya expected. The

high society woman who probably always had perfect hair and nails looked thin, frail, and unkempt. Her smile, however, exuded warmth.

The second she walked into their line of sight, Keith's body tensed and he muttered a curse. Was this a shell of the woman she'd once been?

Amaya was heartsick at looking at Keith's mother, who looked worn down to the core. Not even an attempt at a bright smile could hide the pain and humiliation in her eyes.

She sat down and picked up the phone. Keith grabbed his and reached his free hand toward the glass where he flattened his palm.

"I'd ask how you're doing but..." Keith's voice trailed off.

Amaya couldn't hear his mother's response but she'd become good at reading lips and could get the jest of what she was saying. Tears streamed down the older woman's eyes as she thanked her son for coming.

Her hand disappeared against the glass by comparison to Keith's. His overshadowed his mother's by a longshot.

Amaya could only imagine how helpless he must feel, sitting on this side of the glass. Jackie Firebrand's cheeks were sunken in, and she had heavy bags underneath eyes that lit up as she looked at her son.

"I wish I'd gotten here sooner," he said to his mother, who immediately scolded him. She said she understood and didn't have a right to expect any of her family to show.

The older woman's gaze bounced from Keith to Amaya and then back.

"She's a friend of mine," Keith said before introducing them. He handed Amaya the phone at his mother's urging.

"Hi, Mrs. Firebrand," Amaya said for lack of anything better. "My name is Amaya."

Keith's mother covered her mouth so her son couldn't read her lips. "Please, call me Jackie."

"Will do," Amaya said.

"He's different with you," Jackie whispered as though Keith might hear anyway. "Relaxed. At ease. Comfortable with himself. I've never seen him like this before."

Amaya wasn't sure how to respond so she smiled instead.

"You're special," Jackie surmised. "Keith has never brought anyone home or to meet any of his family."

Amaya didn't think this was the time to point out the fact he'd had little choice. "I feel the same way."

Jackie's eyes sparked and, despite the hand covering her mouth, Amaya could see the woman's smile brightened too. "Take care of him for me, will you?"

"Don't give up on us," Amaya warned. "You'll be out of here soon enough and you'll be able to look out for him yourself." Not that she minded. In fact, leaving Keith was going to be the most difficult thing she'd ever done once this ordeal was over with, and they helped the law locate the bastards behind the attempted poisoning. Plus, she didn't want to make false promises to someone behind bars. It seemed like an extra kick when someone was already down. "I'll let you speak to your son now. It was really nice being able to talk to you."

"Thank you," was all Jackie said, before dropping the hand in front of her face to reveal a wide smile as she turned her attention to Keith.

Amaya couldn't be here in this place without imagining how terrifying it must have been for her nineteen-year-old brother to be locked up in a facility like this one. He'd barely turned nineteen, in fact, when he'd been arrested. She hadn't been able to visit on her own and her dad had refused to go.

Her heart went out to Killian. And yet, she also acknowledged how much a place like this could warp someone's perspective. Being treated like an animal when he was too young and too impressionable.

Killian never spoke about his time behind bars. He never mentioned anecdotes of things he learned. He was dead silent. She'd always assumed he wanted to sweep the experience underneath the rug and forget it ever happened. Move on with his life and figure out how to find work. Find his place in a society that had seen a need to rehabilitate him by sending him into a locked facility with hardened criminals, many of whom were twice his age.

Her brother might be tall but he'd never filled out and probably never would. Despite the jailhouse tattoos he'd come out with and thicker arms, his physique remained much the same as when he'd gone in.

How had his years behind bars changed him? There'd been obvious ways, like he never truly smiled. Sure, he would offer a laugh when she made a joke but it always rang hollow. As did the look in his eyes. Once vibrant chocolate brown eyes turned harder, colder. Detached.

If she met her brother now, would she believe he was capable of trying to kill her for his own gain?

Did her memories of the kid he used to be cloud her judgment to the point she'd become naïve when it came to her brother?

"Of course I'll take care of myself," Keith said into the receiver, jarring her from her deep thoughts. She'd zoned out for the last couple of minutes, lost in her own world. Marky had planted these seeds. Damn him.

Amaya prayed none of it was true. A twinge of guilt took hold at thinking her brother capable of turning on her.

But she couldn't ignore the possibility now that it had been brought to her attention.

"Don't worry about me, okay?" Keith continued. It was beyond sweet that his mother showed so much concern for her son.

"I wasn't there for you when you needed me," Jackie said. Not only did she look exhausted and beaten down but she had an ashen tone to her skin, like someone drying out from alcohol addiction.

Hadn't he mentioned his mother had a drinking problem among other things? Did her brother have an addiction he was hiding? Was that how he'd learned to cope?

Not that it excused anyone's behavior, but it could explain it.

A guard appeared in the small frame. He pointed to an imaginary wristwatch. "Time's up." Amaya read his lips.

Keith didn't immediately move and neither did his mother. It was as though time froze and neither had the will to move.

"Let's go," the guard said as he reached for the phone.

Keith's body coiled, ready to strike. Except there was nowhere for him to go. The partition insured he couldn't reach the guard and he wouldn't be allowed to visit again if he caused a scene.

"We'll come back," she reassured him. "This is only temporary. We'll return before you know it." Her heart ached for both of them.

Jackie hung up first and relented to the guard's insistence she return to her cell. Keith sat there until she was completely gone from view.

"I'm sorry," was all Amaya could say to him.

He turned toward her with red-rimmed eyes that cut her heart out. "Let's get out of here while I can still hold my temper."

Seeing him vulnerable splintered her heart into a thousand tiny flecks of dust. She was all in with the man at this point. Hopelessly in love. A mistake, she knew. But the heart wanted what the heart wanted. All she could do was hold onto a life raft and hope she didn't get sucked under by the wave.

∾

KEITH HELD onto Amaya's hand, keeping a link on the way out of the jail. The link was the only thing tethering him to reality. All he could see was the color red. All he could feel was like the biggest failure of a son. All he could do was hang on for dear life.

Once back in the truck, he white-knuckled the steering wheel and got them on the highway heading north as fast as he could.

"She doesn't look like herself," he said.

"Jail is hard." Amaya might not have firsthand experience but she must have seen what it had done to her brother. "It changes people."

"The messed up part about this whole thing is that she's guilty," he said. "And I wanted to hate her for that reason. I had frustrations with her parenting or lack thereof growing up, but this gave me a concrete reason to dig my heels in. It justified my anger, if that makes any sense."

"It does," she said in a reassuring voice as she reached over to touch his forearm. "Believe me. I spent more than my fair share of time resenting my father. Until I realized I was the one upset all the time. He wasn't around anymore. I'm not saying that I forgave him or want him in my life again. Our situations are different. But holding onto my frustration took away from my own happiness."

Keith sat quiet for a long moment. Those words resonated. Easier said than done. He'd become good at holding onto his anger too. Was it time to let it go? Or at the very least figure out a way to start. Because now he was angry at a system that kept his mother locked up, despite her being guilty.

"Despite the circumstances, seeing her was good," he admitted. More than he expected it to be. In fact, he wasn't sure what he'd expected to find when he walked inside the visitation area. If she'd sat on the other side of the glass pompous, he would have had his answers as to whether or not she had remorse for what she'd done.

Seeing his mother a shell of her former self, stripped of all the makeup and fancy clothes, he felt like he was looking at the real her for a change. She'd had a difficult childhood. Difficult was putting it lightly. And she'd covered up her scars with expensive cosmetics and high-end clothes. She'd hidden behind all those bottles of champagne she'd emptied every night, self-medicating for as long as he could remember.

Now, even though she had dark circles underneath her eyes and her cheeks were sunken in, in some ways this was the healthiest and best she'd ever looked to him. There was only so much that could be hidden. Her demeanor wasn't as stiff and she said more than two words to him, which was another big change. Her smile was different too, genuine. He could get to know this person and like her too.

There was a humility about her now and remorse. Not just for what she'd recently done, but for the mother she'd never been. He'd seen in her eyes and she'd worn it in her expression. There was a kindness he'd never seen.

"I'm glad that I got to meet your mother," Amaya said with the kind of resignation that said their time together would be over soon enough and they would go their separate ways. Her life was in the city and he belonged on the ranch. He could see that now. The thought of striking out on his own held less appeal than it once did. He had Amaya to thank for him coming to the decision to stay put right where he was at and reclaim his birthright.

In truth, the ranch was the only place he was truly happy. Unless he counted being with Amaya. In spite of the extreme circumstances, or maybe because of them, he'd gotten to know the real her in a short time period. They'd learned more about how the other operated under stress than if they'd spent a year together.

Being pushed to the limit had its way of revealing someone's character. There was no hiding the true self when pushed to a breaking point.

Was that the reason many of his brothers and all of his cousins had found true love? None had gone the traditional dating route. They'd all been thrown into sink-or-swim situations with someone, and had come out happier than he'd ever seen any one of them.

Keith gave himself a mental headshake. He wasn't in the market for a wife. So why was he suddenly thinking about Amaya as a long-term partner?

"Everything okay?" Amaya asked, cutting into his revelry.

"Yeah," he said. "Why? What's up?"

"You didn't react to my comment and that's not like you," she shared. He hated that he could hear hurt in her tone.

"Oh, right," he said, fumbling the ball hardcore. "It

meant a lot to my mother for you to be there. I could see it in her eyes." He should probably ask what his mother had to say that was so private she felt the need to cover her mouth but he could venture a guess.

A question tugged at the back of his mind. Did Amaya feel the same way about him? Did it matter when they had an address on Puddin' Pop?

All they needed was an identity and proof she was behind the attempt on Amaya's life. Keith suspected they were about to get both in Richardson.

17

The home on Edgehill Boulevard in Richardson was a small one-story with a worn rocking chair on the porch. Paint was peeling off the siding and the hunter-green shutters looked like leftovers from a 90s themed party. It was the kind of place Amaya thought people might go to buy drugs.

Having stopped on the ride up to grab a couple of burgers from a fast food stop off the highway, it was half past two by the time they arrived. The sun was beating down on them, which caused her to have one helluva headache between her eyes. Food helped.

Keith parked the truck a block away after circling. "Ready?"

"What's our cover story?" she asked, thinking they might need one if someone came asking what they were doing poking around.

"Bible thumpers?"

"Do you think people won't notice if we're not going door to door and don't have a Bible in our hands?" she asked. The religious angle wasn't a half bad idea though.

People would probably slam the door in their faces or close the blinds if they saw them coming.

"It's not election season, or we could go with the angle that we're trying to educate folks about the candidates," he said.

"For a country boy, you sure know a lot about the kind of people who go door-to-door," she said on a laugh.

"Those were the first two that came to mind," he said on a chuckle. "I've heard folks in town complaining about both."

"Do carpet salesmen go door to door anymore?" she asked, figuring she'd throw a few ideas out there too. Being this close to finding out Puddin' Pop's identity was thrilling and scary all at the same time. "Plus, if she sees me walking up, she'll probably take off or not answer the door. She'll know I'm on to her."

"You can always wait here in the truck," he said. "Lay low and let me check it out first to see if she'll answer for a guy."

"She's never met you, so she would be thrown off guard by you walking up to her door." Amaya didn't feel the need to point out how drop-dead gorgeous he was or that most women would be more than happy to receive him as a visitor. If he was a salesman, most would be buying. She'd leave it at that.

"I don't particularly like the idea of separating, but it might be the best option to keep you safe," he said before reaching into his backpack and retrieving a small handgun. "Do you know how to shoot?"

"No," she admitted. She'd never been one of those people who preferred to be outside or shoot a BB gun. Her father sure as hell hadn't taught her the ropes on using a weapon. Killian never had a gun, so him being accused of threatening the clerk with one had been another slap in the face along with additional time on his sentence. "I'm a quick study, though."

Keith showed her the ropes. It didn't take long. "Aiming and shooting while adrenaline is pumping through your veins is the hard part. It'll make your hand shake and that can cause you to shoot wide. I'd advise staying in the truck. In fact..." He pulled the key fob from his pocket and dropped it into the cup holder. "If anyone comes up to the truck, take off. Once I'm out of here, you should scoot over to the driver's seat. Make the adjustments to the mirrors in case you have to get away fast. You'd be surprised at how that can trip you up."

"What about you?" she asked. "I'm not leaving without you."

"I'll be fine," he reassured.

"Then you take the gun," she insisted. "If anyone comes near the truck, I'll drive down the street. If it's an emergency, I'll drive down the street while honking."

He stared at her for a moment. It was easy to see his brain was clicking through the probability she might be dissuaded. He seemed to figure it out when he took the gun she held out.

"It'll be safer with you anyway," she offered. "You know what you're doing and we both know novices end up getting shot more often than not."

"I wouldn't have given it to you if I didn't think you could handle it," he reassured.

"I know," she said. "But you need it more than I do if you're going up to the door."

Keith nodded, before locating an ankle holster and securing the weapon inside. "Here's hoping I don't need to use it."

Amaya held up her burner phone. "Is your phone number in here?"

"It is," he said.

She wasn't sure why that felt so important right now except to say she felt a small tether to him if she could reach him. The connection wasn't much but she'd take what she could get right now. "Call me if you need me to come pick you up."

Not being able to see the home from where they were parked was stressful.

"You got it," he said before leaning across the seat and pressing a tender kiss to her lips. "I'll be right back. I promise."

As much as they both knew he couldn't guarantee anything, she believed him. There was something calming about Keith that was like fresh water in a drought.

Keith exited the truck and then disappeared around the corner and onto Edgehill Boulevard. There were bars on the windows as well as window AC units in cages in the houses where she was parked. She immediately scooted over to the driver's seat and made the necessary adjustments so she could drive on a moment's notice.

The truck engine hummed as she rotated through checking each mirror in case someone tried to sneak up on her. She wished like anything she could have gone with Keith, but that could have made them both sitting ducks. Puddin' Pop would know Amaya on sight.

A thought struck that she hadn't thought of before. What if Loralee had jumped ship and gone over to Puddin' Pop? What if Amaya's former assistant headed into enemy camp? Could the two be working together? Was Loralee in on it?

Probably not, Amaya reasoned. Loralee didn't send the

ugly, threatening texts until after news broke, calling out Amaya as a fraud and a liar about her wholesome lifestyle. At this point, her social media reputation wasn't the thing she cared about resurrecting. She wanted her life back.

Correction, she wanted a life back just not the one she'd had before her world had crumbled. Her standard was higher now. She was done with the smoke and mirrors world of the internet. All she wanted now was a simple life shared with someone she could snuggle up to on a warm night. Prior to Keith, Amaya never slept the whole night with anyone after turning eighteen and getting her own place. Before morning, she would sneak out of her boyfriends' apartments, reminding herself never to get too comfortable with someone. She knew too well those closest to her were the only ones who could really hurt her. Only the people she cared about could truly gut her.

Maybe it took watching her whole life unravel before her eyes in order for her to realize she'd built a house of cards.

One good wind was all it took to blow the house down. There was no strong foundation on which to build, which made the structure vulnerable. Why was everything so easy to see in hindsight?

Amaya tapped her finger on the steering wheel. Patience wasn't her strength. Never would be. She told herself it kept her from ever becoming lazy. Sounded like a good justification at the time.

A man wearing a ballcap stepped out of his home. Most of the houses in and around the block had parking strips or nothing at all. Vehicles dotted the streets. He glanced over her way and then locked on.

Amaya cursed as he changed course, now heading toward her.

KEITH FIGURED the best approach was to walk with purpose, watching that he didn't trip over any of the massive cracks in the sidewalk. He highly doubted that he blended in with his button-down collared shirt but the jeans and boots were a nice touch. They should buy him a seat at any table in Texas. He hoped they worked their magic here too. He was too sharp dressed to be a city worker checking meters and he was drawing a blank trying to come up with another reason to be in the neighborhood.

If the time came, he hoped his brain would kick into gear and supply a decent answer. Being face-to-face with someone while under the gun had a way of getting the ideas rolling.

The sun beat down on the crown of his head as he walked. He wished he'd thought to throw on his Stetson. Maybe he could sell his look better if he looked more authentically Texan. Hell, he was about as Texas as they came.

Then again, being in the city, looking too much like a rancher might make him stick out like a sore thumb.

Keith had no idea how folks dressed here in Richardson. No one was walking around outside. He'd noted on trips to most cities in his home state that folks stayed in their vehicles and minded their own business. Most were in too big a hurry to see past the end of their own nose.

The dilapidated house showed no signs of anyone being home as he approached. The AC unit in the front window encased in black metal bars wasn't running. On a day like today, he figured it would be stuffy inside. There were no opened windows either.

The fact there were no cars parked on the pad or on the

road in front of the house made him think no one was home. This neighborhood wasn't exactly walking distance to the grocery store. He'd noted the distance to necessities on the way in. Someone would need a vehicle to get around.

Although, he thought about all the delivery service options he'd heard about. Apparently, almost anything could be delivered any hour of the day or night in the city. Keith rarely had to leave ranch property considering everything was brought in, and meals were cooked and stored in his fridge. He had no right to complain.

So, maybe someone living here didn't need a car after all. It was possible to be here and not drive. Although, the line of cars parked on the street in and around the neighborhood said most folks drove.

Keith walked right up to the front door and knocked. A cover story still hadn't come to him so he was probably knee-deep in shit about now. He listened for sounds of boards creaking underneath footsteps and heard nothing.

If someone was inside, they were being stealthy. There was no TV sound or light that he could tell from the concrete porch. Blinds were closed at the window unit cage. He hopped off the porch and headed toward the back of the house, figuring it was as good a place as any to head toward next. There was chain link fencing around the back but nothing out front. He slipped into the back without drawing any obvious attention from neighbors. Was this one of the communities where even if someone saw something, they kept it to themselves?

There was a newish shed out back in one corner of the yard. It struck him as odd considering the age of the home. Wouldn't someone put money into fixing up the place they lived versus where they housed yard equipment? He made a mental note to check it out before he left. The doors were shut so he didn't see an emergency need to head that way.

The backdoor was as non-welcoming as the front. Instead of a screen door, there was metal. No lock, which struck him as odd. Wasn't that the point of having this kind of security?

He checked around the backyard for signs of dog droppings. The last thing he needed was to be surprised by one of those bull breeds that kept quiet until you breached their home. Even then, they just handled the situation rather than alert the neighborhood.

Keith didn't want to run up against one of those even though he'd always been told he had a way with animals. There were no droppings and the grass was equally patchy. No yellow spots from the ammonia in dog urine either.

To the best of his knowledge, no animal lived here.

There wasn't any sound coming from the back of the house either. Human or otherwise. Which could mean he'd been spotted and was being watched. He checked around for any signs of cameras or home security systems even though he doubted this home was paying to have their home professionally monitored.

What was there to steal inside?

Drugs came to mind. He could almost see this place as a meth lab for how broken down and seedy the place looked.

He risked trying to look inside from one of the windows. Blinds were drawn. Whoever lived here didn't want anyone peeking in, that was for sure. It would be easy for the person inside to see out though. More than that, Keith had a creepy-crawly feeling as he poked around the place. Something felt off but he couldn't put his finger on it exactly.

Keith tried the back door. It was locked.

The place looked similar to every other house in the

neighborhood except for the lack of a vehicle. Granted, this home was unkept. The neighbors had pride in their homes. They neatly manicured the lawn or kept up with the paint.

At least several of them did.

This home was on the end of the street. To one side was the back of a parking lot of what looked like a junkyard but he supposed was a car repair shop of sorts. One that maybe specialized in hard to find parts and then fit them into cars. If he was a betting man, he'd put his money on the business owner buying stolen vehicles, parts, or both.

Which didn't make the whole neighborhood a bad place. It was a mixed bag.

Since he couldn't get a good look inside, Keith figured he'd head back to the truck to check on Amaya. Being apart made him nervous. Not because she wasn't capable of taking care of herself. She was strong and independent and had been doing a helluva job since long before he came into the picture.

Except the threat this time was the real deal and her life could hang in the balance. He hadn't heard any tires squealing, so he took that as a good sign. Still, he couldn't shake the hairs-on-the-back-of-his-neck-prickly feeling.

Was someone watching him?

Possibly from a neighbor's house? It was possible he showed up when the owner was visiting someone across the street. Or next door.

The tiny needles pricking his skin feeling returned. Keith circled back to check the shed. As he neared, he saw the lock had been tossed on the ground.

18

Amaya considered her options as the man in the ballcap neared. For a split second, she wished she'd taken the gun. At the moment, she was torn between putting the gearshift in drive and gunning the engine or staying in her spot like a sitting duck.

The man's chin was to his chest, no doubt to avoid directly looking at the bright sun. Her imagination ran wild anyway. She couldn't make out the details of his face.

Based on his general size and build, he didn't ring any familiar bells. She tightened her grip on the steering wheel with her left hand and dropped the right to the gearshift. It was too late to change gears without drawing attention.

At the bed of the truck, he stopped. Her heart battered the inside of her ribcage.

Ballcap barely glanced in her direction before checking the mail. It was too soon to give a sigh of relief, considering this could be a ruse to throw her off. No way would she let her guard down.

After pulling out a stack of envelopes, he circled back in the direction he came. He could have decided to check the mail at that moment because there was a 'suspicious' truck parked close to his house. He might have been on a mission to memorize her license plate in case he needed to call it in.

But he didn't appear to be out there to cause harm. So, she exhaled.

A question loomed. Where was Keith?

He'd been gone for a solid fifteen minutes. The walk to the house couldn't take more than three or four. Double the number for round trip and he'd been gone six to eight minutes. That left more time than she was comfortable with for him to be investigating the house.

Was he invited inside? Were they barking up the wrong tree? Anything was possible.

An old Corolla turned down the street, coming up from behind. She glanced in the rearview mirror. Panic struck as she slid down in the seat and bent over as the vehicle passed so the driver wouldn't see her.

No way. It couldn't be him.

~

KEITH STOPPED and listened at the door of the shed. It was bigger than the average backyard shed used to house lawn mowers and yard equipment. This one had been rigged for Keith to be able to stand up inside.

He reached for the door, stopped mid-reach and changed his mind.

Keith bent down and retrieved his handgun. He palmed the weapon and removed the safety, just in case. There was a reason cops led with their guns pointed directly in front of them, and not to one side. A good shooter knew on instinct the few seconds it took to raise a gun could mean the difference between life and death when walking into an unknown situation.

Barrel leading the way, he reached for the door with his left hand and then swung it wide open.

The garage was set up like the studio Amaya had shown him belonging to Puddin' Pop. This was the place.

However, it was empty. He'd believed someone had run to it in a hurry. Did someone run out instead, not taking the time to lock up?

It would take a high degree of confidence that no one knew about this place to pull off such a move. Or desperation. Or someone who was a little too comfortable they wouldn't get caught.

Keith stepped inside the studio to see if there was anything lying around that might identify the owner. The place was staged with white blankets hanging on the walls. They would make it easier to put up a fake background. Although, weren't there filters now that could essentially do the same thing?

He wasn't into taking selfies or distorting his image, but he'd heard others talking about how easy it was to change their appearance online with all the tools available on phones nowadays. Bridget owned the most popular beauty shop in town and was the cheapest place for a men's cut. He'd heard her and her patrons yacking it up, having fun with filters while he waited his turn in the chair. Bridget had insisted on showing him some of the results, which were always good for a laugh.

In the right-hand corner as soon as he walked it sat a small table with a makeup mirror plugged into an electric cord. He followed the green cord, noting it ran to the house. How had he missed that before?

A large cosmetic bag was unzipped, much of its contents

spilled out onto the tabletop. A selection of wigs sat on one side. A garment rack was to his left with a variety of costumes. He walked over to check them out. The sizes were larger than he expected them to be, based on the videos he'd seen of Puddin' Pop.

Then again, the camera could distort most everything about a person, including their shape. There were apps Bridget used to make herself look skinny.

He picked up one of the garments and held it up. A man small in stature could fit in this. Between the makeup, wigs, and apps, he could see a situation where a man was pretending to be a woman.

To gauge the reaction, Keith pulled out his phone and texted Killian the address. Told him to meet in the shed out in the backyard.

Three dots immediately appeared indicating Killing was typing a response.

The dots disappeared.

No message.

Some texts took a minute to come through depending on the cell tower and how much traffic there was. That was the case in the times he went to Austin for a weekend. Then, there was weather. Cloudy days seemed to make signals weaker.

He waited.

Nothing.

Lighting was plugged into an electrical strip and aimed at the opposite corner of the room. This place had everything needed to host a channel. Except an occupant. He walked over to the corner to check it out.

Out of nowhere, the shed door swung open. Keith's back was to the door. He swiveled around a few seconds too late.

A male stood there, aiming a gun at the center of Keith's chest.

"Put your hands up where I can see," the familiar voice said. Now, he could put a face to the voice.

Keith did as ordered. The shooter had a clear shot at point-blank range. He didn't have to be a good shot to hit the target. "What are you doing here, Marcus?"

Marcus seemed momentarily taken back by the fact Keith knew his name.

"Put the gun down. Slow. Or I'll blow your brains out," Marcus said.

"You don't want to do that," Keith said as calmly as he could. "It would be too messy. Plus, the noise would alert the neighbors. Someone would call 911 and you'd end up in jail."

Marcus was roughly five-feet-nine-inches with a slight build. His black hair was slicked back and his skin was pale. He looked like a deflated Superman. But he fit Puddin' Pop to a T. He fit the costumes. He fit the wigs. He fit the character.

But why betray someone he called his best friend?

"You're a good talker," Marcus said. "But, like, it's over now. So, what I'm going to need you to do is put the gun down. Not that it's your business but there is nothing here to connect me to Puddin' Pop. I made sure of it. The cops can pick your brains off the walls and never link me to this god-forsaken place. I'll be long gone before they show up anyway. And, believe me, they take their sweet time answering calls in this neighborhood, honey. I don't live like Miss Thang does. Living in a penthouse while refusing to take me with her. I deserve everything she has and more. Why does she get to have everything while I live here? It's always been like that too. Even at the restaurant. Her tips were bigger than mine. I worked my rear end off. I gave better service. Do you think people noticed?" He shook his head as his face turned red from anger. "I'm better than that bitch at everything we do. I should be the one living in the lap of luxury, not her. She might have a sob story about her childhood but doesn't everyone? Now, put your damn hands up."

Keith held up his hands so Marcus could see them clearly even though he wanted to throw a punch at the bastard. The last thing he needed was a nervous shooter with a twitchy finger. He also realized Marcus was going to have to kill him to keep his secret life. Would he risk doing it inside his studio space?

Halfway down, a female figure stood at the opened door behind Marcus. The sun was to her back but he would recognize her silhouette anywhere. Speak up and Marcus would spin around and shoot her most likely, after he fired a bullet at Keith.

Amaya, no!

⁓

AMAYA HAD TO THINK FAST. She was still trying to process the fact someone she called her best friend at one time could attempt to steal her business, let alone drug, defame, and attempt to kill her. This whole scene was a nightmare and she had to think fast.

She'd picked up a broken concrete block on the way across the yard, needing something to use as a weapon. If she used it now, Marcus could accidentally shoot Keith.

At this point, she realized Marcus was going to kill Keith anyway. He was most likely trying to think up the least messy way to do it.

Keith was halfway to the ground with his weapon. She

needed to move fast if she was going to give him a chance to pull up and shoot.

It occurred to her that Keith most likely wouldn't attempt a shot while she was in the background.

There was no time to analyze best moves. She had to throw Marcus off his game and give Keith a chance.

"What the hell are you doing, Marcus?" she demanded.

As he spun around to check behind him, she chunked the block at his skull and then jumped to the opposite side of the door.

Keith took her cue, rolled out of the way, and then came up with a solid shot.

The last thing she saw as she jumped out of view was blood splatter from Marcus's hand and the gun he'd been holding go flying.

∽

KEITH TUCKED his body into a ball, and then rolled into Marcus's legs like a bowling ball slamming into pins. He heard a crack, possibly a shin bone breaking from the force of the hit, and a grunt as Marcus lost his balance.

The man was already screaming about his bloody hand. Something about losing a finger. Panic set in and Marcus started screaming and kicking like a banshee.

Marcus was no match for Keith, who easily put him in a wrestling hold.

"Say goodnight, bastard," was the last words Marcus would hear before being choked out.

The next thing Keith knew, he was looking up at a concerned Amaya.

"There's blood all over your shirt," she said, dropping down beside him with concern lines etched in her forehead.

"It's his," he said. "Not mine."

Relief was a tidal wave of emotions crossing her features as tears streamed down her face.

"I called 911," she said. "Cops are on their way."

As if punctuating her sentence, sirens sounded in the distance.

"You were brave to do what you did," he said. "You saved my life."

Amaya shook her head. "That's where you're wrong, Keith. You saved mine from the moment we met."

The sirens blared, indicating the cops were out front.

"Hold on," Amaya said as she put her hands in the air and gaited toward the sound.

Not a minute later, a pair of beat cops in Richardson uniform came around to the back yard. Amaya didn't come with them, causing a wave of panic that she might have been saying goodbye a minute ago.

Keith stood up and turned Marcus over to one of the cops as an EMT joined them. He gave his statement to the cop's partner as the EMT bandaged Marcus's hand. He came to screaming and kicking, which netted him a shot of some kind that made him a whole lot more cooperative.

But all Keith could think about was Amaya.

The officer thanked Keith before taking down his information for the file, questioning him about the shooting, and taking his gun as evidence.

"Am I excused?" Keith asked.

The officer said he was, so he headed toward the front of the house. Halfway across the yard, Amaya and Killian turned the corner. Killian had his arm around his sister, comforting her like a good big brother.

As they met, Killian handed her over and said, "She's all yours now. Take good care of her."

"You'll always be my big brother, Killian. And I will always need you in my life," Amaya said to him.

Killian smiled through red-rimmed eyes.

"We are always in need of smart folks at the ranch," Keith said to Killian. "How do you feel about living in a small town."

"For a good job, I'd move to Timbuktu," Killian said with a half-hearted laugh. His eyes said he meant those words. "I got computer certification while in jail. Any chance you could use help with your online operations?"

"I'll check with my family but most of us like being out on the land," Keith said. "We can always use smart folks in the office."

Amaya beamed up at Keith, and his heart was done for.

He looked Killian in the eyes. "Normally, I'd take you out to dinner before I asked this question. I have no idea how Amaya feels so I might be barking up the wrong tree. But someday, when your sister is ready, I'd like to ask her to marry me. I've fallen head over heels in love and I can't imagine living another day without her. What I'm saying is that I'd like your permission to ask for your sister's hand in marriage."

Killian's smile was wide. "You have my blessing."

Keith turned to Amaya, took her hand in his, and got down on one knee. "Amaya, I don't know what stroke of luck brought you into my life. But I'm deeply, madly, wholly in love with you. I can't imagine my life without you in it but I understand if this is moving too fast for you. If you need to take time to evaluate—"

Amaya was shaking her head as she pulled him up to standing and put her index finger over his mouth to stop him from saying another word. "I don't need a ring and I don't need you to get down on one knee. I'm yours, Keith. I love you more than I can ever imagine loving anyone. And I'd like to spend the rest of my life getting to know you, growing better together. So, if you need a ceremony to prove we're in this forever, I'll do it. But all I need is you."

Those words were all it took for Keith to loop his arms around her waist and pull her closer. He kissed her, tenderly at first. His beautiful Amaya. His life. His home.

When they pulled apart, Killian came in for a group hug.

Keith's heart was full. He'd found something he never knew he was searching for. He found his heart.

19

EPILOGUE

Travis Firebrand couldn't believe his brother, the baby of the family, was engaged to be married. What was this world coming to? Never mind. He didn't want an answer to that question considering their mother was in jail and their father was a complete mess. The world was bonkers right now. Ever since his grandfather's death, the ranch had been in turmoil. Long before, if Travis was being completely honest.

Forgiveness didn't come easy to Travis and the betrayals were racking up. He would ask how life had become so complicated but it most likely always had been. He'd been too young and invested in his own world to notice.

At twenty-seven, he was the second youngest brother and cousin out of the eighteen combined family members. The number of single Firebrands was down to two. Technically, his older brother Kellan had been married once, short-lived as it had been. The marriage to Liv had been a mistake on her part. The divorce so she could marry Corbin, Travis's cousin, had added fuel to an already blazing fire.

To his cousins' credit, no one seemed to blame Travis's

side of the family for their mother's attempted murder. That was no small miracle. Travis wondered if he would be so forgiving if the situation were reversed. But then, his side of the family tree had always been accused of being the bad side.

What did that even mean?

He couldn't argue his parents were messed up. But then so was his Uncle Brodie. Aunt Lucia was the only decent parent on either side of the family. In his estimation, she was a saint. Travis would rather be on the circuit than here at the family home. The circuit meaning rodeo. But everyone needed to work the ranch and come together.

Travis almost laughed out loud. Kellan might put up a pretense that everything was fine but underneath the surface his blood boiled. Travis could see a storm brewing. He just had no idea how bad it was going to get.

Speaking of storms, what was Brynne Beauden doing roaring up the driveway in an old Chevy with a shotgun hanging out the driver's side window?

TO KEEP READING, click here.

ALSO BY BARB HAN

Texas Firebrand

Rancher to the Rescue

Disarming the Rancher

Rancher under Fire

Rancher on the Line

Undercover with the Rancher

Rancher in Danger

Set-Up with the Rancher

Rancher Under the Gun

Taking Cover with the Rancher

Firebrand Cowboys

VAUGHN: Firebrand Cowboys

RAFE: Firebrand Cowboys

MORGAN: Firebrand Cowboys

NICK: Firebrand Cowboys

ROWAN: Firebrand Cowboys

TANNER: Firebrand Cowboys

KEITH: Firebrand Cowboys

TRAVIS: Firebrand Cowboys

Don't Mess With Texas Cowboys

Texas Cowboy's Protection

Texas Cowboy Justice

Texas Cowboy's Honor

Texas Cowboy Daddy

Texas Cowboy's Baby

Texas Cowboy's Bride

Texas Cowboy's Family

Texas Cowboy Sheriff

Texas Cowboy Marshal

Texas Cowboy Lawman

Texas Cowboy Officer

Texas Cowboy K9 Patrol

Cowboys of Cattle Cove

Cowboy Reckoning

Cowboy Cover-up

Cowboy Retribution

Cowboy Judgment

Cowboy Conspiracy

Cowboy Rescue

Cowboy Target

Cowboy Redemption

Cowboy Intrigue

Cowboy Ransom

For more of Barb's books, visit www.BarbHan.com.

ABOUT THE AUTHOR

Barb Han is a USA TODAY and Publisher's Weekly Bestselling Author. Reviewers have called her books "heartfelt" and "exciting."

Barb lives in Texas—her true north—with her adventurous family, a poodle mix, and a spunky rescue who is often referred to as a hot mess. She is the proud owner of too many books (if there is such a thing). When not writing, she can be found exploring new cities, on a mountain either hiking or skiing depending on the season, or swimming in her own backyard.

Sign up for Barb's newsletter at www.BarbHan.com.

Printed in Great Britain
by Amazon